Murder at the End of the World

By Jonathan Garrett

[jonathanagarrett.wordpress.com]

Cover by: Meghann Pardee [whatakuriosgirl.blogspot.com]

City of Illdara

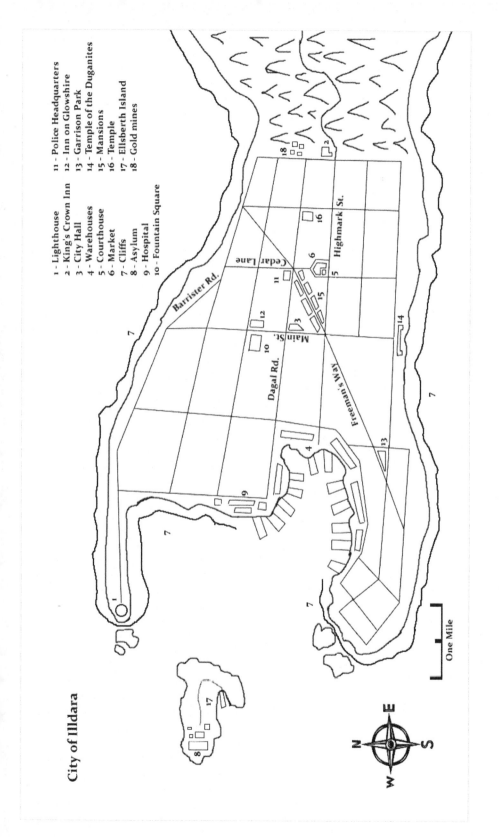

1 - Lighthouse
2 - King's Crown Inn
3 - City Hall
4 - Warehouses
5 - Courthouse
6 - Market
7 - Cliffs
8 - Asylum
9 - Hospital
10 - Fountain Square

11 - Police Headquarters
12 - Inn on Glowshire
13 - Garrison Park
14 - Temple of the Duganites
15 - Mansions
16 - Temple
17 - Ellsberth Island
18 - Gold mines

Barrister Rd.

Cedar Lane

Highmark St.

Main St.

Dagal Rd.

Freeman's Way

One Mile

N
W
S
E

Chapter 1

Murder. The word had spread like a mid-summer wildfire through the capital, where there certainly was no shortage of killings. The rumors started with a rider come up from Illdara, a city at the tail-end of the world. They spread to the darkest alleys, they spread to the wealthiest manors. That word soon was on the tongue of commoner and noble alike, speaking of the subject as if it were some new and unusual thing.

This killing had not been a theft turned murder, where the perpetrator hastily tried to cover up his crime after the fact, nor was it the swift and clean kill of an assassin paid a high price to have someone gotten out of the way. It bore the marks of a crime of passion, if 'passion' was truly the right word. A flood of raw emotions, an unthinking act of sudden and brutal violence, the evidence left where it fell.

But there were hints in the rumors and sketchy reports, hints that the killing had not been quite so sudden. It was no ordinary crime of passion, a jilted lover or spurned suitor driven to a murderous rage. Something else was in play: premeditation, planning. This heinous act was carried out over an extended period of time and with a meticulousness that only someone who'd killed before, and didn't mind killing again, would engage in. Planned violence...it made no sense.

Nevertheless, that was what Allison Newberry, newly appointed as detective, had been able to gather from the scant details that had made their way out from Illdara through the first week.

It was not because of these bizarre details that "murder" had been so widely uttered. One fact alone had put the word on everyone's lips: the victim, a thirty-two year old woman named Victoria Celeste, who had been in Illdara for a brief stay. A wealthy socialite, often seen at parties dripping with jewels and gold, and wife of the minister of finance. Perhaps if she'd been someone else, this matter could have been swept under the rug and eventually forgotten. But the rumors soon spoke of how her husband had broken down in the middle of a cabinet meeting upon hearing the news from a young page. His cries of anguish and shouts for justice had been heard echoing throughout the halls.

So *someone* had to go and make sure justice was delivered.

Allison sat with her arm against the sill of the open window of a carriage, staring into the cold fog that hung thick in the canyons east of Illdara. Strange patterns swirled and danced as the coach rushed through the still air. The echo of the horses' hooves was hollow and strange, bouncing off the unseen peaks on either side the road. Bells on their harnesses jingled faintly, just at the edge of hearing. Two days of this, with no more than a few hours to rest each night. Her pocket watch showed just after eight o'clock; only one more hour of riding through that miserable clime and she'd be able to put all the jostling and bumping behind her.

"You'll be in front of a fire at the King's Crown before long, Miss," the driver called back to her. He was an aging man, almost completely bald, but with a steady hand that had grown strong from holding the reins of his team for countless years. He'd taken this trip a hundred times before, at least, and could likely make it blindfolded, if he ever had need to. There was about him the air of a man for whom the world held little excitement and few surprises, he'd seen all this world had to offer. "Is this your first time all the way out to the edge of the world?"

"First time, yes," Allison replied.

"Aye, I've seen a lot of your type, then. Everybody's got their reasons, eh? Maybe it's the wrong one, maybe it ain't, but they got their reasons. You're a detective, aren't you, Miss?"

"Something of the sort," Allison said, listening to the conversation with only halfhearted interest.

"Never seen a female detective before. Kind of strange they'd send you all the way out here, if you don't mind me saying so."

"I'm here *because* I'm a woman."

The old man seemed to ponder this for a moment. Then he laughed. "Well, no matter, no matter. Illdara will chew you up and spit you out just the same. I've seen it before, Miss, many a time and no mistake about that. But you'll be fine, I suspect. It's the ones that've got 'baggage,' you see, they're the one's that have it bad. You can run from a man who means to do you harm, but you can't run from your own past, your own memories. Some people think they can, think that Illdara's far enough to get away from somethin' they seen or did. Well...maybe it is. For some of them."

Observations like that were probably part and parcel with ferrying people along the only road between civilization and Illdara, a city as isolated and as lonely as any you were likely to find, if the stories held true. On all those trips he'd probably seen thousands of different people. Some coming and some going. Would she appear any different to him when she left? Did she appear any different from all those others to him now? It was a gloomy atmosphere into which Allison ventured, no mistake of that.

Soon the fog parted at last, revealing the city of Illdara. Only it still clung too thick to see beyond more than a dozen or so blocks of dull, gray buildings, as lifeless and solitary as the mountains they'd just come through. A welcoming sight it was not.

The driver slowed the carriage as they approached the first structure on the widening road. A sign hung loosely near the front door, gently swaying back and forth, proclaiming it to be the "King's Crown Inn." The building was an old one, made entirely of wood and saved from rotting in the cool, moist air by an act of the gods and liberal use of preservatives. It seemed to sag inward on itself, as if a weight were pressing down against its roof. A number of repairs had been made to various parts of the inn, a new wall here and a new window there, making it appear something of a hodgepodge of disparate materials cobbled together over many long decades.

The inn, being at the eastern edge of the city, was still very much a part of the mountains, and so provided a panoramic view of the entire city from its highest windows, at least as much of the city as could be seen in that forsaken fog.

The carriage stopped directly in front of the main door and the driver came around to let Allison out. She stepped down and stood on solid ground again, having long since tired of the constant rattling of the carriage on its stiff, wooden wheels.

"Welcome to Illdara, Miss, tail-end of the world," the driver said, his toothy grin showing off several missing teeth. "Enjoy your stay here."

With no more said to her, he returned to the driver's seat and then carefully turned the carriage around, pointing back towards Trenton.

"You're not going to wait for any passengers?" she asked him curiously.

"If they're not here by now," he said, "they're not likely to be. This is the last carriage out before winter. A few more days, a week at most, and the snow'll be thick enough to keep out even the king's army." He tipped his hat in her direction. "I'll see you again come spring, if you can make it that long."

The driver whipped the reins and the horses leapt forward. The carriage was swallowed up by the fog.

A man came through the front door of the inn, approaching Allison with carefully measured steps and then saluting with a crisp grace once he'd reached the proper distance. No wasted movement whatsoever. His high-collar, wool coat, peaked helmet, and polished, copper badge clearly marked him as a member of the local police force. His stance and demeanor marked him as a strict professional, in every sense of the word. A wooden truncheon, about seven inches long, hung loosely from the thick belt around his waist. That seemed to be the only weapon he carried. Given his height and build, it was probably the only one he needed.

"Yore the deetective, aye take it?" he asked, his accent thick with eastern intonation. A man far from home, it seemed.

"That's right," Allison replied. "Allison Newberry, junior detective in the King's service. It's good to meet you, sir."

"Cahnstuble Nigel Wilminson," the officer said.

They shook hands briefly. The constable's hand quickly returned to his side.

"Aye have been tahsked with die-recting you to police headquartahs and helping you find yore way 'round town. Should you need a thing at ahl, I'm the one to ahsk."

Allison nodded, even as she struggled to keep up with him. "That's good, I'd wondered if I'd be left to fend for myself once I got here."

Constable Wilminson, despite his professionally-stiff shoulders and erect form, eyed the flintlock pistol peaking from behind Allison's unbuttoned frock.

"I assume that my being armed won't be an issue?"

"No, Deetective," the constable said, "it won't."

Allison was, nevertheless, left with the impression that it was an issue, but Constable Wilminson said no more about it, instead motioning for her to follow him further along the street into the city proper. Allison's bags were left sitting unattended near the front door, where she hoped no one would bother them.

No carriage had come to pick them up, nor had any horses been provided, leaving the two of them to walk the streets of Illdara like two beat cops. The experience would at least give her an opportunity to get a feel for the city, what it looked like and how its layout affected the movement of its people. All of that might have nothing at all to do with the murder...or it might have everything to do with the murder. Allison always kept her eyes sharp. She was, after all, her father's daughter.

Illdara, pressed from the east by the Thorall Mountains, on the north and south by sheer cliffs that dropped down to raging, rocky waters, and on the west by the icy Nimball Sea, felt very cramped and very small. Staring at maps could not adequately convey just how it felt to actually stand in those streets, knowing with absolute precision just how far it was to the nearest town big enough to have a name. That distance was considerable.

The fog, though thinner than up in the mountains, still made its presence felt and obscured everything starting two or three blocks away. Although the King's Crown Inn was little more than a league from the docks, and of a much higher elevation, she could see nothing at all of the latter. As they walked further into the city, the street became more crowded, though even at its worse it seemed quite calm and orderly compared to the noise and confusion of the capital less than a week ago.

The buildings on either side of the street were sturdy, but plain, bearing few adornments beyond informative signs and the occasional painted shutter or curtain. It would not be entirely correct to call the city austere, but Illdara did come very close to achieving that descriptor. The impression was amplified by the looks she received from all the people they passed. No glowers or glares, the people just stared outright as she walked by, tilting their heads slightly for a closer look and not bothering to make the move appear casual. If the constable noticed that they had suddenly become the center of attention, he made no mention of it, nor was there any sign about his professionally-blank face to suggest that he knew or cared.

Illdara was...different. The carriage driver had spoken rightly, it was as far from the rest of world as you could get and people oftentimes went there to get away from problems, both of the mental and physical variety. But it was not a place traveled to lightly, nor was it traveled to with any great frequency. Illdara was the sort of place that people didn't talk about. Those who lived there rarely left and those who merely visited were often tight-lipped about the experience upon their return, if they ever spoke of it at all.

Much of the city's history was a blank slate, save for several accounts of major invasions and sackings. It spoke to the resilience of Illdara's people that the city still thrived despite such violence. No one knew for sure when the city had been founded, though some were willing to claim that it was at least four hundred years old. The main export was gold, which came from thick veins in the mountains and was stock-piled during the long, winter months. And that was all that one could know without actually going there.

"Have you lived her long, Constable?" Allison asked.

"Neah to twenty yeahs, Deetective," the constable said, still looking straight ahead.

"What brought you here? If you don't mind me asking."

"Aye came suhching for something."

Allison hesitated for a moment, wondering whether it would be at all polite to ask further. "Have you found it yet?" she asked, her curiosity overriding her politeness.

"No, Deetective, aye've naught yet found it."

After about a mile of walking east on the carefully-placed cobbles of Highmark Street, Constable Wilminson turned to the north, where they passed through a large, open-air market. Venders from all over the city were selling a wide variety of wares beneath a mass of cloth tarps and hastily-erected awnings. The low din of commerce that drifted up from the market was muted and orderly, lacking in the shouting and arguing that was expected of such a place. It was familiar even so, evidence that life existed even in this dreary place.

Allison was struck by how calm and orderly everything seemed to be. There was no pushing or shoving, no shouting or carousing. Even the streets themselves were largely free of trash and debris, and they were all as straight as a knife blade. Order to that degree didn't come about by chance.

At last they came to Illdara's police headquarters, a multistory building dotted with small, thick windows. The entrance was a pair of stout doors that looked sturdy enough to fend off a crowd of angry rioters. But for the lack of an outer wall, it could easily have doubled as a fortress. The constable opened one of the doors and motioned for her to go inside.

"Chief Inspectah Jairyn 'as his office near the back, right cornah," the constable said, pointing in that direction. "He can tell you ahl about the muhduh."

"Thank you, Constable," Allison said, "I'll go see him now."

A number of wooden desks had been placed throughout the main room, some of which were currently occupied by officers filling out reports or examining bits of evidence collected in one crime or another. Many of them glanced out of the corners of their eyes in her direction, the same looks she'd received from the townspeople. She walked past them to the corner of the room, where she found a door with a neat, metal plaque that stated "Chief Inspector Blaire Jairyn." Allison tapped lightly on the door.

"Come in," came the muffled response.

The room beyond was tiny and cramped, heaped up with an assortment of articles, ranging from personal trophies of solved crimes to weapons that could easily have been a century old. A broadsword, of the kind used by the military before the advent of firearms, stood in a corner with its tip resting on the tile floor. Inspector Jairyn stared at her through an opening in the stacks of documents that weighed down his desk.

"Ah, Detective, how good of you to come," the inspector said very smoothly after the briefest of hesitations. "You'll have to excuse the mess, I rarely see visitors here in my office. Today is an exception, I'm afraid. I'd have cleaned, but..." He made a motion that took in the entire room. Any attempt at cleaning would have taken hours, as well as extra space to store some of the larger articles. Both were likely in short supply. As there was no place to sit, aside from the chair that Inspector Jairyn was already using, Allison stood near the center of the room, hands clasped behind her back.

"I came as soon as I was able to," she replied. "The journey here is no short one, believe me."

"We are quite some ways from the rest of the world, yes."

The inspector stood, then, and Allison got her first good look at the man. He was in his early-thirties, perhaps not quite a decade older than herself, and had golden-blonde hair that was neatly trimmed and perfectly straight. He could easily be thought of as handsome, though that was partially dampened by the stark severity of his eyes and the obvious aura of self-assurance bordering on arrogance. The look on his face carried the story of his career every bit as well as the plaques and awards on his wall ever could. Chief Inspector Jairyn had solved a number of very difficult cases in his career and would solve a great many more before he was done. It put the present murder in a much different light.

"I'd like to get down to business right away, if you've no objections?" Allison asked.

"Yes, yes, of course. I can understand that you'd like to get to work immediately and get this case solved. We feel the same way, believe me. This case has...brought scrutiny down on us from the other cities, scrutiny that we could all do without. Privacy is something we hold dear here in Illdara, that's often why people come here. There's none of the problems of the outside world, none of the noise and confusion. People can live quietly and simply. As long as this murder remains unsolved, all that is threatened."

An invasion of the city's privacy, their most prized possession, by an outsider. She might as well have been breaking into their homes and making off with their valuables, was what the inspector was hinting at. Then it was not only the inspector's professional reputation on the line as long as this case remained unsolved. Inspector Jairyn picked up a small stack of documents from a drawer in his desk and held them up.

"This is everything that we've managed to uncover about the case," the inspector said.

Allison quickly flipped through the files, enough to get a feel for the nature of the attack and the state of the scene, but not deeply enough to get mired down in the details just yet. There would be plenty of time for that later.

"What can you tell me about the victim herself? Specifically, the nature of her visit and what she was doing around town."

"Well," said the inspector, "we know that Victoria Celeste was here on business and met with a number of people during her stay. From what we can gather in talking to those who saw her, she was looking into trade routes in and out of the city."

"Her husband is no merchant, what reason would she have for this information?" Allison asked.

"That, I can't say," the inspector said with a flippant shrug of his shoulders. "Have you not talked to her husband?"

"He was interviewed before I left," Allison said, idly tapping the stack of documents against her open palm, "but the minister of finance was, unfortunately, not overly close to his wife and rarely meddled in her personal affairs. Their relationship was somewhat complex, as I understand it."

"I see," the inspector said curtly, "then that gives us nothing with which to work."

"May I see the body?"

The inspector shook his head. "I'm afraid that won't be possible. We did what we could to preserve the body, but the damp climate here makes that difficult. We had her cremated yesterday morning, as decay had already begun to set in."

"What of the scene?"

"Ah," the inspector said, brightening, "now that is a different matter entirely." He stood up and gestured toward the door. "Lead the way out, we shall go to the scene directly."

Chapter 2

The scene, a narrow alleyway not far from the docks, had been left in its original condition since the murder nearly nine days ago. A bright-red strip of cloth had been run from one side of the alley to the other in two places, leaving a twenty-foot section closed off from the public. Allison leaned over the cloth and looked down at the hard-packed dirt.

It was no different from any other alley, being narrow and unfriendly and not the sort of place that a proper lady would find herself, unless brought there physically or through clever guile of some kind. Faint bootprints dotted the dirt in the alley, but they appeared, at first glance, to be not too dissimilar from the boots commonly worn by half the populace. The local police had taken care not to leave any prints of their own, at least.

"Were there any witnesses to the crime?" Allison asked.

"Unfortunately not," Inspector Jairyn replied. He stood a few feet behind Allison, giving her room to work. "Mrs. Celeste was discovered some time later by a homeless man, who practically fell over her. We believe that's where the set of bootprints you are currently inspecting came from."

"When was she found?" Allison asked, easing under the red cloth. She was careful to only put her boots down on solid rock, where she would leave no marks of her own.

"About an hour past midnight, it was reported almost immediately."

"And the time of death?"

"We can't be sure of the exact time," said Inspector Jairyn. "Madam Celeste left a social gathering approximately two hours before midnight, leaving us a window of three hours in which the perpetrator may have carried out his attack."

The attack had been a violent one, this much was clear just from looking at the way that dried blood was spattered thick across one side of the alley. It had pooled against the wall, where the woman had fallen. She'd practically been bled dry.

"Have you discovered the weapon?"

"No, we searched the alley from one end to the other and many of those nearby, but turned up nothing. From the wounds, we believe that it was a large knife, very sharp."

A beautiful young lady of the upper class, murdered in a most violent fashion in the middle of a dirty, ill-used alley. Though Allison's experience was limited, having been on the police force for only three years, she knew enough about the workings of the profession and the workings of the world to realize that there was something about this that didn't feel right. Inspector Jairyn had been forthcoming about all information related to the crime, and the evidence she could gather from seeing the scene itself supported that, but her mind refused to accept that such an act could have been borne solely of a sudden passion.

"Had Madam Celeste ever traveled to Illdara before?" Allison asked.

"Not to my knowledge, Detective Newberry," the inspector replied. "This seems to have been her first trip here."

"What about friends? Does anyone here know her very well?"

Inspector Jairyn thought on this for a moment. "She met with several families during her stay here and they all readily accepted her into their homes, but I think that due more to her position than to any sort of friendship. Have you thought of something?"

"Perhaps," Allison said. "An attack of this nature, being as violent and bloody as it is, bears the hallmarks of a crime of passion, a sudden burst of anger or hatred, even jealousy. Yet, as you say, she had no real friends here and had only been to Illdara this one time. Would such a short stay have been enough to engender such emotions in her killer?"

Inspector Jairyn turned and leaned against the wall of a building, his arms folded across his chest. "The facts of this case just don't seem to add up," he said. "We considered it might be, as you say, a crime of passion, but have been unable to uncover anyone who might have been close enough to her to commit such an act." His head turned slightly, looking at her out of the corners of his eyes, and his voice lowered. "I'll tell you now that I don't like having an outsider come in and do my work for me. Not at all. But if it means solving this case as quickly as possible, then I am willing to swallow my pride. For the time being." He pushed away from the wall. "I'll have all the case information and what evidence we have sent to your room at the King's Crown Inn."

Allison was left alone at the scene. The isolated, insular nature of the city had raised its head once again. Inspector Jairyn had not been angry, not exactly, but her presence in Illdara was clearly unwanted. Mrs. Celeste had been an outsider, as well. Perhaps, being of Illdara, he'd not been able to see it properly. Their unknown perpetrator might have had similar ideas about outsiders and had taken that view to an extreme. "You aren't wanted here," the message read, inked in blood and spread from the tail-end of the world all the way to the capital. If such were true, then this one act might only be the first.

She continued her search of the scene, but found nothing of note that the local police had overlooked. With little else to be gained there, she let her feet take her through the streets and lanes of the city, idly wandering.

Though many of the buildings had multiple stories, they were all very blocky and squat. Windows were always small and uninviting, walls were square and corners sharp, and there was very little in the way of parks or open squares to liven things up. In fact, she'd seen very few trees at all since entering the mountain pass several days ago. Illdara was a cold city, even without the bitter, northern winds that stung Allison's face and hands.

People continued to watch her everywhere she went. None approached her and none called out to her, they simply watched as she walked past. It was an eerie feeling to have so many sets of eyes watch her every movement. Was it because she was an outsider? Or because everyone was on edge over a detective from the outside coming into their isolated world and digging into their lives? There was no way to be sure without talking to them directly.

Allison spotted an old woman sitting in front of a bakery, a paper bag clutched firmly in her wrinkled hands. She made no move to get up and leave as Allison approached.

"Could I speak with you for a moment?" Allison asked.

"What about? I don't have all day to flap my gums."

"Have you lived here in Illdara long?"

The woman's eyes narrowed. "Why do you want to know that?"

"I'm new here," Allison explained. "I only just arrived today and I'd like to know more about the city, if I can."

"Nothing to tell," the old woman said, standing up. She clutched the bag tighter than before. "We're ordinary folk. Don't need no outsiders trying to stir up trouble where there ain't none." She turned and scurried away, as quickly as her thin, brittle legs could carry her. Allison watched until she disappeared around a corner.

She turned to see her reflection in the bakery window. Her clothes were plain: a dark frock with a wide collar over a buttoned waistcoat and trousers of an equally-dark color, standard uniform for detectives in the capital. They differed slightly from the more utilitarian style of dress common in Illdara, though not by a great deal. She was still wearing her pistol, partially obscured behind her frock, but had certainly given no indication that she meant to use it. And nothing of her pale, smooth skin or dark hair, which lightly touched her shoulders, suggested malice or ill-intent of any kind, at least that she could tell. Yet that old woman had looked at her as someone might a common pickpocket. No, even a common pickpocket would likely get more respect than that.

Though the sun moved ever higher, the steel-gray clouds in the sky kept the city shrouded in dim, ambient light. The fog lingered well into the day.

Back at the King's Crown Inn, which Allison had returned to after tiring of constantly being the center of attention, she found the common room on the bottom floor nearly empty. The barmaid, cleaning a table in the corner, flashed her a brief smile. That was the first Allison had seen all day, excepting the carriage driver's crooked grin.

"Would you like anything?" the young barmaid asked. She'd be pretty if not for the sweat that beaded on her face, her rumpled, too-small clothes, and the limp, stained dishrag she held in one hand.

"Later, perhaps," Allison replied politely. "I'd like to go up to my room first."

"Of course, of course," the girl said. She went around behind the bar and took a key out from a locked cabinet on the wall. She handed over the key with another brief smile. "Inspector Jairyn said to give you a room for as long as you need. It's on the fifth floor, third on the left."

"You know Inspector Jairyn?"

"Oh yes," the girl said, bobbing her head. "Everybody knows him." She leaned in close and lowered her voice. "He's very famous. Why, they've heard about him all the way at the capital!"

"Thank you for the room."

Four flights of creaky, groaning stairs curled upward. She'd have much preferred one on the second floor and, given the scant number of customers on the bottom floor, there should have been one empty there. But the expense was not coming from her own pocket.

"Bloody hell!"

The exclamation brought Allison out of her thoughts. She looked up to see a man in the hallway on the fifth floor standing in front of one of the doors. He had a key in his right hand and a deep scowl on his face. He kicked the door roughly with his boot.

"Do you need something?" Allison asked calmly.

His glare carved its way through the hallway before falling on her. "Pike off!"

18

If not for the glower on his face, he'd have been fairly handsome. He had the squarish jaw, broad-shoulders, and sandy-blonde hair that were not unlike those of the men commonly portrayed on dime novel covers, but with just a touch of softness to keep him from crossing over into the absurd. His clothes were common: long, brown pants with suspenders crawling up and over a stout shirt whose sleeves were rolled halfway up his forearms.

Allison pushed back one side of her frock to reveal her flintlock pistol. The man stood transfixed by it for a moment, before fully realizing what it meant.

"Look," he said, his anger suddenly drained, "this is my room, hey? I paid for it and everything. But this bloody key won't turn the lock."

Allison pushed him aside and tried to turn the key. Just as he'd said, it wouldn't turn a bit. She grasped the handle of the door and pulled it up as hard as she could. The aging wood groaned and shuddered, but the lock turned.

A sigh exploded from between the man's lips. "I've already been up and down these gods-forsaken steps a half-dozen times. Thank you very much."

"Are you a traveler?" she asked.

"Sailor," he said. "Came into the docks a few hours ago on a steamer. Probably be one of the last to make it into the harbor before it all freezes over, least that's what they told me. I'll be wintering here, whether I care to or not. You?"

"I came through the mountain pass this morning," she said. "It'll be full of snow in a few days."

"Ah, you're like me then, hey?" He chuckled to himself. "Well, it'll be nice having a neighbor from out of a town to talk to, the people here don't seem overly sociable from what I've seen."

That was certainly an understatement.

"As a fellow outsider, what do you make of this city?" Allison asked.

"A queer place filled with a queer people," he said, grinning without humor. Then he shrugged his shoulders. "They have reason, perhaps. Illdara has been sacked and plundered all of four times in the past three centuries, so they say, by invading armies and even invading merchants. A history like that would surely tend to make people...suspicious."

"I suppose that's true enough," Allison said, "yet I can't help but feel there may be more to it than that."

"Perhaps there is, love, but it's not something an outsider like you or I could ever hope to understand." The man pushed the door to his room open and stepped inside. As the door slid slowly closed, he looked over his shoulder. "But do be careful, love, much goes on in this city." The door shut and the latch clicked.

Allison went to her own room, the door to which she found much easier to unlock. The room was small, with nearly half the floor space taken up by a long, narrow bed and the ceiling no more than a hand or two above her head. The curtains on the window--gray, like everything else-- were pulled back, letting in the dull light of a cloudy, winter day. Her bags were sitting just inside the door.

She took off her frock and threw it over the back of a nearby chair. Her holster went next and then she sat down on the edge of the bed. It was comfortable, if not overly soft. Adequate for the purpose it was designed for, but you wouldn't scramble to get one for your own home.

The city through the window looked little different from what she'd seen on foot. Gray buildings, gray streets, pressed closely together on all sides. A town that small in size, with so many people, ought to have been crowded every moment of every day, but it seemed not to be. There was not the press of that sea of humanity as it moved in all directions at once, nor were the streets full of carriages, carts, and horses as other cities she'd seen had been. Either a great many of the buildings in Illdara were empty or its citizens, for the most part, stayed behind their doors.

The man she'd met in the hallway had spoken rightly, Illdara was indeed a queer city. Somehow, someway, she'd have to navigate its streets and alleys to find the answer to a question that even its own people couldn't solve. Allison lay back on the bed, still wearing her waistcoat and boots, and fell asleep.

Chapter 3

At midnight, a bell tolled. Allison sat upright in bed as the sound echoed throughout the city, bouncing off the mountains to the east. Twelve tolls in the dead of night. Echoing. Echoing. Allison went to the window and looked out at the city. A few lights scattered about in a sea of darkness, mostly gas lights that burned along the sides of the streets until morning came again, though she could see candles glowing faintly in a few windows. The streets and the sidewalks were all empty, not a soul was out and about at such a late hour.

She briefly considered returning to her bed, but the sound of the bell and the cool night air that came in through the window had awoken her fully. Her mind was already working and she felt that longing to make some use of her time.

The common room had more men and women in it at midnight than earlier in the day. They were all either drunk or rushing headlong towards it, as ale and other dark brews flowed freely and were as quickly consumed as they were poured. Many seemed travelers, like herself, though not all appeared to be. Perhaps some of the locals preferred the drink of the King's Crown Inn, or else were there for other reasons that were less obvious.

Allison chose an empty table in a corner of the room. The barmaid came around with a tankard, which she placed on the table without being asked to do so. Allison took the tankard and raised it to her lips. The dark ale was frothy, and had a deep, malt flavor heavy with the sharp bite of hops. Alcohol was not her preferred drink, but she'd sipped enough in her time to know that this was of a particularly high quality. With nothing else to do, she continued to drink the ale while she watched the rest of the common room.

There was chatter, light and friendly. It was difficult to pick out specific conversations, but it was clear from the mood that nothing of a serious nature was being discussed. She saw none of the stares and suspicious faces that she'd seen outside the walls of the inn, but then, they were inside the only place she'd seen so far that catered to those from elsewhere. Perhaps this was where the two sides met, to get to know one another and to shake loose the preconceived notions that bound them out in the streets. Allison finished up her ale and set the tankard aside.

As she went to stand, the barmaid approached again.

"I'm so sorry, Detective," she said, handing Allison a large, leather satchel. "Inspector Jairyn told me to give this to you the next time you came around. I'd have taken it up to you straight away, but we just go so busy that I didn't have the time."

"Thank you," Allison replied, taking the bag. She opened it and spilled its contents out on the table. All the evidence taken from the scene and all the reports that had been written up now lay spread before her. There was a purse, and a small, leather bag which held all the contents taken from it, a coin pouch that still jingled with coins, and a few other personal articles. Among the reports was a detailed drawing of the scene itself, including the position of the body when it was found, and a full account of the state of the body written down after it was taken to the coroner. Once she'd examined the reports, she set them aside and poured the contents of the purse out onto the table.

Various cosmetics, the likes of which any proper lady would always have close at hand, a small hand mirror, and several articles of jewelery. As with the coins, they'd not been taken following the attack, excluding robbery as a possible motive. Allison sat for a moment and stared down at the tiny pile of personal effects. This was all that was left of a young woman's life. A few trinkets, a few baubles, a few coins, nothing of particular import.

Amidst the pile, something caught her eye. She brushed away some of the larger articles and picked up what appeared to be the head of a match, red and unburned. There was nothing particularly strange about it, being merely a match head like any other. But what would Mrs. Celeste have been doing with it? There was no evidence that she smoked and it was unlikely that she was the sort of person to go around lighting candles or fireplaces. A woman of her social standing would certainly have someone else do that for her. Of course, it could just as easily have fallen into her purse in any number of places. It might have no bearing on the case whatsoever.

Allison gathered up all of the loose articles and put them back in the bag. She returned to her room on the fifth floor and went directly to the window. A bright, nearly-full moon lightly touched it's own shimmering reflection, which was tossed and battered by the rolling waves. All the clouds that had hung low over the city were completely gone and she could see down to the docks, past Ellsberth Island, and all the way out to the sea and beyond. Every half-minute, without fail, the powerful beam of the lighthouse's light would sweep across the city, casting strange shadows that danced from rooftop to the rooftop. As she watched it turn, her mind tried to make some sense of the case.

24

When morning came again, the fog had returned just as thick as it had been the previous day. The cold air from the north and east meeting the warmer air and water from the south likely meant fog most mornings. The temperature had also plunged since the day before, dropping well below freezing. Down in the common room, Inspector Jairyn was waiting for her. He lightly touched the brim of his stout cap.

"Good morning, Inspector," she said. The barmaid came around and offered both of them breakfast, which consisted of two eggs--scrambled--and a slice of toasted bread lightly brushed with butter. The two ate in silence.

"I'd like to speak with the coroner," Allison said once the meal was finished. "His professional opinions might help me make some sense of the evidence at hand."

"Certainly," the inspector replied. "I can take you there immediately."

The coroner had his office in a small building adjacent to police headquarters. The interior of the building was dark, lit by a few stray candles that illuminated two rows of metal tables bearing bodies covered in white sheets. The air was thick with the stench of death and preservatives and was very cold, seeming to be even colder than outside. Each breath that Allison and the inspector exhaled came out as a puff of white smoke. The coroner himself, a small man with thick glasses, stood over one of the corpses with scalpel in hand. A candle burned by his side, giving him just enough light to see by. He did not look up from his work.

"Conley, do you have a moment?" the inspector asked.

"Not now, Inspector Jairyn," the coroner said, irritation in his voice. "I am busy now, come again later."

"I've brought the detective, the one who came from the capital. She would like to speak to you about the murder some two weeks ago. The young, foreign woman?"

The coroner finally looked up from his work. He stared at her with his blue, bespectacled eyes and Allison felt a shiver run down her spine. The man might as well have been staring at another corpse waiting to be dissected. He set the scalpel down.

"What do you wish to know?"

"Whatever you can tell me," Allison said. "But we can start with the nature of her wounds."

"Twenty-two stab wounds," the coroner said, reciting from memory. "All ranging from half-inch up to two, jagged edges."

"Jagged edge? An old, rusty knife, perhaps?"

"No," said the coroner. "Serrated knife. Ornamental, perhaps, still sharp."

"Was there any sign of a struggle? Any defensive wounds?"

"A few slashes across her hands and wrists, but not many. Attack, perhaps, came sudden and victim was already dead, or close to it, before realizing that anything was happening." He shook his head slowly. "Poor woman."

"Is there anything else you can tell me?"

The coroner thought for a moment. "Ah, one thing more. Don't know if this thing will mean much to you." He fished around in his pocket for a moment and then produced a small, leather pouch. Allison took the pouch and upended it. The head of match, red and unburned, fell into her open palm.

"Where did you find this?" Allison asked.

"In examining wounds," the coroner said, "found this few inches beneath skin, believed it might be important to case."

"It might be," Allison said, staring down at the match head. She looked up and turned to Inspector Jairyn. "How many places in the city are there that make or sell matches of this kind?"

"A few," the inspector said, shrugging his shoulders. "Is it important?"

"There was another match head in the contents of Mrs. Celeste's purse."

The inspector's eyes widened slightly. "You're right. I'd forgotten all about that! I can get that information soon enough from the archives. Was there anything else you wanted to ask about?"

"No, we're done here."

At the main building, Inspector Jairyn enlisted the aid of a few of the other policemen in digging through the archives. It took them all of two hours to find what they were looking for: a listing of all the manufacturers and sellers of that kind of match. It was certainly incredible that they had such detailed information available.

According to the archives, there was one manufacturer operating near the harbor and three stores scattered throughout the city that sold matches of that kind. It was not particularly popular. Allison gathered the various sheets of parchment, containing addresses and names, and prepared to leave. Inspector Jairyn stopped her.

"I had the homeless man brought to the station," he said, "the one who found Mrs. Celeste's body. I thought you might like to talk to him."

"Lead the way," Allison replied.

His name was Bradley Ahls, according to his own testimony, an aging man who'd spent most of his life as a homeless beggar, due in part to a clubbed right foot that left him unable to do even the kinds of work that a man of his limited intelligence would be relegated to. He looked up as Allison entered the tiny room that he'd been brought to. She felt suddenly very cold as he stared, unblinking, his eyes oddly dull and lifeless. His jaw hung slack, mouth half-open.

"Mr. Ahls, they tell me that you discovered the body of Victoria Celeste some two weeks ago. Is this correct?"

"Yeah," he said, "found 'er all dead like. Lotta blood."

"What were you doing in that alley?"

"Walkin'. Just walkin'."

"Did you hear any kind of struggle or see anyone else that night in the alley?"

His arms slowly wrapped around his chest and his gaze dropped to the narrow table in front of him. His voice became little more than a whisper. "Nothin', didn't see nothin'. Just blood. Lotta blood."

"Did you contact the police immediately after you found the body?"

"Screamed," he said. "Just screamed, and they came."

The poor man had neither seen nor heard anything beyond the discovery of the corpse, but that alone seemed to have been more than he could bear. Continuing to poke and prod him with questions would not elicit anything useful, and the man himself was likely better off being allowed to forget what he'd seen that night.

"Are you finished?" Inspector Jairyn asked.

Allison nodded and several officers came to lead Bradley away. He did not look up from the floor as they walked him out of the room, nor did his hands cease in their trembling.

The harbor of Illdara, covering most of the eastern edge of the city that was not sheer cliff, was far more alive than anywhere else. Broad-shouldered men with strong hands, bare from the waist up even with the temperature well below freezing, walked this way and that, some hoisting massive crates by cable up to ships and others carrying barrels of food or drink. Several dozen ships clung to the three and a half miles of grasping, wooden fingers, flying flags from more than half the countries of the world. They were all waiting for the first shipments of gold from the deep mines in the mountains, waiting for the spring thaw.

The watchful eyes of the local police stared from every street corner and many of the ships still appeared to have the bulk of their crews on board. Even here, where the races and nationalities of man co-mingled, there was that same suspicion. Allison kept this observation to herself.

They arrived at the address found in the archives around noon. The building had planks nailed across the front door and the shutters were closed tight. White paint peeled from the walls in great strips, to be blown away by the wind from off the sea. No matches had been made there in a long time.

Inspector Jairyn frowned. "It has been some time since we last updated the information in the archives, but a closure like this should have made its way in."

Allison walked up several stone steps to the front door. The planks had been attached with nearly a dozen nails each and there were six in all, slightly askew. Whoever had sealed it up had not meant for it to be easily opened again. The two searched the exterior of the building, but found no signs of any forced entry.

"I supposed we could force our way in if we had to," Inspector Jairyn said, "but I doubt we'd find anything. No one's been in there for months. We may have more luck in visiting those stores."

The three stores, each approximately a mile apart, were general stores that sold a variety of goods the public might have need for. Dried food was chief among what they sold, but other household items, including matches of different kinds, were also in abundance. Two of the three shop owners could recall nothing at all of that particularly type of match and merely shrugged their shoulders when Allison showed them the match head. But the third remembered.

"Ah," the aging man said, idly smoothing the front of his white apron. "We did have some of those back--oh--a year ago, maybe? Never did sell all that well, now that I think of it. One day they just stopped coming."

"What can you tell us about these matches?" Allison asked.

"Well, they're fairly water-proof," the shop owner replied. "You can get 'em all wet and they'll still light up, won't bend or nothin'. Most of the time it was the sailors that bought 'em, since they're always out at sea. But they never did buy enough."

"Do you have any of them left?"

The shop owner scratched the back of his head. "Ah, no, I'm afraid not. I had three boxes of twenty back a month or two ago, but someone came in and bought 'em all."

"Someone?" Inspector Jairyn asked. "Tell us what you can remember."

The shop owner grimaced. "I don't know," he said. "Just someone. A man. Ordinary, I guess."

"Surely-" Jairyn started to say, but Allison put her hand on his shoulder and stopped him.

"We won't get any more information here," she said. Then she turned to the shop owner. "If you can remember anything else, please come to police headquarters immediately. Until then, have a good day."

He dipped his head in their direction as they left.

"That was our last lead," Inspector Jairyn said, arms folded across his chest.

"For now," Allison replied. "But we did get some good information today, I think. Enough to have something to work with later."

Inspector Jairyn checked his pocket watch. "There's some work that I need to attend to back at headquarters. You will excuse me, I hope?"

"Certainly, I can find my own way back to the King's Crown."

The inspector lightly touched the brim of his hat and then left. Allison was alone in the city once more, with nothing for company but the suspicious stares of the locals and the gentle cry of sea birds as they drifted overhead. She watched as a flock of them curved through the air and then swooped down towards the harbor, looking for a place to light.

If it was true that the sailors who often came to port were fond of those matches, then perhaps she would have some luck in talking to them. And as she was as foreign as they were, perhaps they might be more willing to talk to her. Especially without Inspector Jairyn peering over her shoulder.

Chapter 4

"Can't ya see I'm busy right now?" a burly sailor asked. He carried one barrel on each massive shoulder and appeared as though he scarcely realized they were there.

Allison showed him the copper badge that she usually kept hidden in her pocket. He looked at it for a moment. She wasn't entirely sure that he could read what it said, but its intention was, nevertheless, quite clear to him. He let out a rough sigh and set the barrels down. He then proceeded to sit on one of them. Allison hesitated for just a second before sitting down on the other.

"Alright, what do ya wanna know?"

She showed him the match head. "Do you know anything about this kind of match?"

"Sea match," he said immediately. "You see them around sometimes because they can work even when they're wet. Not much call for 'em these days, though."

"Why not?"

His broad shoulders rose slightly, then fell back into place. "We just bring our own, I guess. Look, I'm no expert on which is better or why, I just use whatever's around. If you wanna know why we have one kind and not the other, you'll have to ask the captain. He's the one who decides that. You need anything else?"

"No, that will be all."

"Good."

Once Allison had vacated her barrel, the sailor grabbed up both and wandered off back towards his ship.

She spent two hours stopping every sailor who was willing to be stopped and asked them all about the matches. Each time she got the same unhelpful answers. They were just ordinary sea matches. Some could recall seeing them, but not particularly often. No one could recall anyone having a specific interest in them. She even managed to pry a few words out of a ship captain, who was overseeing the unloading of cargo from his ship, but he didn't even recognize the match head when she showed it to him. Allison walked slowly north, pondering her next move.

"You're not from around here are you?" The words were quiet, almost a whisper. An old man was sitting not far away beneath an awning, his face shaded by the wide brim of a hat. Smoke drifted up from a long pipe he held between his teeth. His skin, weathered and wrinkled, looked more like tanned leather than proper skin, an intricate map of a long, wind-tossed life. He was the sort of man people had in mind when they used the term "old salt."

"Is it that obvious?"

The old man nodded. "Nobody's even got to hear you to know that. They can just look at you, you've got the look of woman who's never set foot on these streets or seen these buildings before."

"Is there something you need from me?"

"Nah," he said, "nothing like that. Just wanted to tell you a few things before you walked on by." He tipped his straw hat up just slightly, so that she could see his eyes. They were milky-blue, blind or very close to it. "You ought to leave while you can. One day you'll wake up and it'll be too late."

Allison frowned. "I don't understand what you mean."

After a bought of wheezy coughing, he spat roughly on the sidewalk. "I don't expect you to, girl, but it's the truth just the same. People that come here, they don't leave so easily, hey? Not if they stay too long. It ain't the kinda thing you can explain to somebody, but you'll feel it just the same. I feel it, too, every hour of every day. That pull, the hands that grab you 'round the arms and legs and never let go. Some days you feel it more than others, but you always feel it."

Allison gave him a measured stare. "I've no intention of staying here longer than I have to," she said. "I've a job and a life back at the capital and little desire to give up either."

"Maybe," he said, unaffected by her words or her tone. "Maybe. I heard more traveler than one say that very thing. Even I said it once, a very long time ago." He spread his arms. "Look where it got me." Then he chuckled a dry sort of chuckle, rough and humorless. "You gotta be tough, girl, and you gotta know who you are. That's all that can save you in this forsaken city."

The old man continued to puff at his pipe, but it was clear that he had exhausted his desire for conversation. He didn't even turn his head to watch her leave.

Allison spent much of the rest of the afternoon continuing to harass the sailors who happened to be away from their ships and generally being as much of a nuisance as possible, but got no usable information for her efforts. No one to track down, no address to look up. Just vague, halfhearted responses from them all.

It was frustrating. The whole situation was frustrating, not just the case itself. The capital could have sent an entire team of investigators and policemen to take this matter in hand and get it solved. But instead they'd chosen her, a junior detective, because it was a case that no one else wanted to deal with. Sending a team had been dismissed immediately, as it had been deemed likely to offend Illdara and its people.

It was true, of course, but all the dead ends, suspicious stares, and narrow, unfriendly streets were simply more than Allison was prepared to handle on her own. After a full day spent inside the city, she hurried back to the King's Crown Inn and sought out the relative safety of her room.

The sun had not yet set when there came a light rapping at her door. Allison sat up in bed, almost convinced that she'd simply imagined it. But the sound came again.

"Come in," she said, quickly smoothing some of the wrinkles out of her clothes.

The door opened to admit the young man who stayed in the room opposite her own, whom she'd met the day before.

"Hullo," he said, briefly raising one of his hands.

Allison tilted her head in his direction. "Do you need help getting back into your room?"

The man laughed at that. He had a kind sort of laugh, unreserved. "No, no, nothing of the sort! It's just been too long since I've had a nice conversation with anyone. Not that I have anything against the people here, mind, but they tend not to be the greatest of conversationalists, especially if you happen to be from the other side of the mountains."

"I've noticed that myself," Allison said. She motioned towards an empty chair near the bed, which the man gratefully took.

"I haven't introduced myself yet, have I?" he said, looking a bit embarrassed by that fact. "Martin Roundtree, by name."

"Allison Newberry. You've likely realized by now that I'm a detective."

"Yes, I thought so! It's quite rare to see anyone else walking around with a pistol hanging from their belt." He paused for a moment and stared towards the window. The curtains were pushed back, so that it was possible to see all the way down to the docks now that the fog had mostly cleared. "This city...it's very strange, don't you think?"

"It's certainly different from the capital."

"I've never been there before," Martin said. "Is it really as beautiful as everybody says?"

"I've always thought so," Allison replied. "Sun-dappled parks awash in the flowers of spring, broad lanes lined with trees, or the summer festival when all the town is dressed in the brightest colors. There's simply nothing to compare it to. I've only been gone a week and half and already I miss it more than I can bear." She paused. "Though truly, I can only speak of it in such wonderful terms because of how different Illdara is. Not all that I know of the capital is so...happy."

Martin smiled faintly, just a barely-seen turning up of the corners of his mouth, as though he understood more of the capital than just a few wistful tales. "Someday I'll go there," he said, "when my work here is finished. That's my hope, anyway. That's my hope."

"When this whole business is through," Allison said, "I might just take you there myself."

His smile this time was neither so faint or so brief and Allison was glad to see it.

"Perhaps you may, love. I'd certainly enjoy traveling there in the the company of such a lovely young woman as yourself. Of course, we'll have to wait until that old man and his coach come back through the mountains and that's certainly not to happen anytime soon."

Allison sighed. Though she'd just spoken so highly of the capital, two decades of memories were quickly staining that nostalgic vision. "A week away from the capital and already I've forgotten how anxious I was to get away. I've stories enough for an entire winter, Martin, so you may yet decide to travel elsewhere."

"Oh, I'm sure it's neither so good nor so bad as your memories tell you it must be," Martin said. "I know well enough what it's like to long for a place and time, to at once run towards it and run away from it." He idly ran one hand lightly up and down along the suspenders that looped over his chest. His eyes focused on the floor about halfway between his feet and the window. "Illdara's the kind of place that really makes you think about things, love, good and bad. The things you want to get away from, the things you want to hold close. I want to leave after just a few days, but then I start to think about all the things out there in the world that I've seen that aren't quite so wonderful. And I think maybe I should stay a while longer."

"I've already been warned about such a thing," Allison said.

"Oh?"

"An old man, at one time a foreigner in Illdara. He told me not to forget who I am or where I came from."

Martin nodded. "Sage advice," he said. "Well, I'm not overly interested in spending the rest of my life here regardless. Why settle for Illdara, when I can have the whole sea to myself?"

They continued to talk for a while, of nothing particularly important. Allison told Martin more about the capital--though she avoided digging too deeply into matters best kept to herself. And Martin told her of a life at sea, oftentimes at the mercy of such a tempestuous mistress. It was nice just to talk to someone again, even if she'd only just met him the day before. He had that quality about him, an openness that could draw you in and make you want to stay for a while.

Martin stood at last. "Sorry for taking up your time like this and humoring my desire for a bit of friendly banter. Good day, love." He bowed his head slightly and then left. The door clicked shut behind him.

Four days passed.

Chapter 5

Morning light, such as it was, brought with it a low muttering that filled the common room, replacing the somewhat cheerful banter that Allison had heard there before. Inspector Jairyn was late in arriving, so Allison ate alone. Just as she was finishing her meal, the front door of the inn opened. Inspector Jairyn stood in the doorway, a vicious scowl sewn onto his face. He spotted her in the corner and curtly motioned for her to follow him outside. Allison hastily thanked the barmaid for the meal and then rushed out into the cold, morning air.

Inspector Jairyn stood beside a carriage, its horses breathing heavily, with his arms folded across his chest. "There's been another one," he said flatly.

"Another one?"

"Another murder. Almost exactly in the same manner as the first."

"What?!" Allison exclaimed. "When?"

"We found the body less than an hour ago at the mouth of an alley, the entire scene has been roped off for now and no one, not even my own men, have had a chance to look at it. If you would kindly hurry, we can be at the location in only a few moments."

Not wasting any time, Allison got into the carriage. Inspector Jairyn motioned to the driver and then got in on the other side. The horses lurched forward, jostling the cramped carriage, and they rushed west into the city.

The scene was along the northern edge of Illdara, in an alley that stared out over the sheer cliffs, which dropped down more than a hundred feet to the angry, foaming sea below. Allison quickly got out of the coach once it had stopped and followed Inspector Jairyn through the crowd that had gathered to gawk at the scene. At the head of the crowd was more red cloth, this time creating a perimeter around the mouth of the alley. It was further bolstered by a line of uniformed policemen, their arms spread wide to prevent any curious onlookers from getting too close. They parted to allow Inspector Jairyn and Allison past.

"It's your scene," he said. "See what you can find."

The alley this time was cobblestone, like the road, meaning no footprints unless the killer had been unlucky enough to step in a pool of blood. Unfortunately he, or she, had not. The victim was an old man and Allison realized after a few moments' study that she'd seen him before. It was the same old man whom she'd talked to down at the docks. She'd not recognized him immediately on account of his face having become contorted into a rictus of pain and from the bloom of crimson across his throat. For good measure, the assailant had stabbed the poor man at least a dozen times more. Or else his throat had come last. Either way, he'd been long dead before the attack was over.

Allison pulled on a pair of thin, leather gloves and then carefully began searching the old man's clothes. She found several coins in his pocket, a few coppers and one piece of silver. All had been left behind, the same as with Mrs. Celeste. She also found his pipe, still sharp with the smell of burnt tobacco. There was naught else in his pockets but lint. The killer might have made off with something, but they would have no way of knowing. An ordinary robber, however, would not have left the coins.

Her attention was then directed to the scene itself. The blood that pooled up to an arm's length from the body was entirely undisturbed.

Aside from the cobblestones, the second scene looked much the same as the first. An ill-used alley, the body left somewhere near the entrance. No attempt had been made to hide it. Everything she'd seen so far suggested that it was most likely carried out by the same person. But there was one more thing she needed to check.

Allison carefully pealed off her gloves. They'd gotten smeared with blood, so she handed them to one of the policemen at the perimeter and asked him to have them cleaned for her at his earliest convenience. He nodded his agreement and placed the gloves in a leather pouch.

"Has this man been identified yet?" Allison asked.

"Albert Brimley, a local vagrant. No permanent home, though he's been known to frequent the docks begging for coin or doing what odd jobs his advanced age allowed him to do."

"The spurned lover of a noble would have little reason to slit the throat of a homeless man, I'd think. Perhaps he knew or saw something, but I happened to speak with him just a few days ago and he made no mention of Mrs. Celeste or who might have killed her."

"Indeed," the inspector said. If he was shocked to learn that she knew the man, he didn't let on. "Are you done here?"

"Yes, I've seen enough."

"Good, we can get the body to the coroner and let him handle it from there."

Allison nodded. "I'll be going with the body."

"What?"

"Is that a problem?"

The look on the inspector's face suggested that it was, but he instead made a grumbling sound in his throat and turned away. "Whatever you think best."

The policemen pushed the crowd back further as another carriage arrived. Men in white clothes came out and carefully put the body of the old man on a stiff-backed stretcher. Once he was settled, they pulled the flaps of material that hung from either side up over his body, covering him from view. They then carried the body to the carriage and placed it inside. Allison grabbed hold of a handle on the back of the carriage and pulled herself up onto a metal step.

As the carriage bumped along the cobblestone road, Allison's mind was at work. If the first murder had been to send a message, what message did this second murder send? Albert Brimley had lived in Illdara many years, enough to have become integrated into the city's culture, far more than it seemed he'd ever wanted to. Was it because he'd spoken to her, warned her of the city's bizarre dangers? She'd not seen anyone around when they'd spoken and the people of Illdara hardly seemed like the type to gossip. This second murder only served to muddy the waters even further. If these two murders were indeed by the same individual, it would be up to the coroner to provide the next clue.

The coroner watched dully as the orderlies brought in yet another lifeless body for him to examine. It was the kind of thing that he'd done a hundred, perhaps even a thousand, times before and Allison got the impression that he only ever viewed those bodies as a puzzle to be solved, and any living person as a puzzle waiting to happen.

His assistants appeared shortly after the body arrived. They were both young boys, somewhere in their early teens, perhaps, and twins. The coroner pulled back the flaps of material, exposing the body of the old man. He then bent over the body and gently lifted the hands, inspecting them carefully. Even the underside of each fingernail was checked.

"No sign of defensive wounds," he said. One of the assistants scrawled a few things on a sheet of paper. The other was already deep into drawing a perfect rendering of the corpse. "All blood under victim's fingernails is his own."

He set the hands back down and then looked over the torso. The old, ratty clothing was soaked through with blood and so clung tightly to the skin. The coroner cut through the fabric with a pair of scissors and exposed the bare skin to the air. "Jagged entrance wounds, like woman from approximately two and a half weeks ago. Ceremonial dagger, most likely, serrated." He paused, then. "Throat slit, different blade. Clean cut." The assistant continued to write.

Allison cleared her throat, hoping to catch the coroner's attention. "Would you say that this was most likely done by the same person, Mr...ah...I don't believe I ever caught your name?"

"What?" the coroner asked, suddenly realizing that there was a fourth person in the room. "Conley," he said absently. "Conley. Yes, same person. Probably. Some differences exist, but too many similarities, as well. Details have not been released to public, perpetrator has knowledge of case that most do not."

"What about the throat?" Allison asked.

"Odd," Conley said. "Very odd. First victim was not killed in this manner, and throat here has clean cut. Penetrations came from same style of blade on both, but not throat."

"Why do you suppose that's the case?"

Conley tapped his blood-smeared fingers against his chin as he stared at the far wall. "No way to know from information available." He turned back to the corpse. "Will now examine wounds for...foreign object."

This was what Allison had been waiting for. Only Conley, perhaps his assistants, Inspector Jairyn, and Allison herself knew that the head of a match had been discovered in one of the wounds on Mrs. Celeste. If they found another in this body, as well, it would be the proof they needed to say for sure that they had a serial killer on their hands.

The slow, tedious process of carefully cleaning and then examining each of the near-two dozen wounds took more than an hour. Allison stood on the tips of her toes, watching over Conley's shoulder for even the slightest hint that he'd found something that didn't belong.

On the last wound, the nineteenth, Conley paused with his fingers more than an inch into the wound. He pulled his hands out and picked up a pair of tweezers. Allison's breath caught in her throat. The tweezers plunged into the wound and dug around, probing the soft flesh. After a moment, they retreated. Between the two metal tongs of the tweezers was the petal of a rose.

"It's not the same," Allison heard herself say.

"Very strange," Conley said. He picked up a glass eyedropper and carefully washed away the blood from the delicate petal.

"Why a rose petal?" Allison asked. "Why anything at all?"

"Clues," Conley said. "Both are clues, guiding us. Arrogance, perhaps. Taunting us into following him. Log it." His assistant scrawled yet more. He held out the tweezers with the petal in them. "I am not flower expert. Take to market just south of here. Will inform Inspector Jairyn of findings when he arrives."

"Thank you, Conley," Allison said as he dropped the petal into her palm. Washed of the blood, it had a deep purple hue that went all the way to its root. The coroner and his two assistants had already returned to their work and were no longer aware of her presence. Allison left the dimly lit interior of the morgue and returned to the gray skies of Illdara.

The open-air market, which she'd seen the first day, was every bit as busy as it had been then. As she walked past dozens and dozens of stalls, the locals, possibly without even thinking about, eased around her, avoiding even the most incidental contact. They at least did not glare at her anymore, but being ignored entirely was almost as bad.

Allison searched every vendor that sold flowers, of which there were a few, looking for one selling purple flowers. Even with temperatures dropping below freezing during the night, they still had flowers for sale, as odd as that seemed. They were all of a hardy, northern stock, though still beautiful in their own right.

One such stall was operated by an aging woman whose yellow teeth had not been clean in a good, long while. She sat hunched over her wares, watching with dull-eyed indifference as hundreds of potential customers quietly filed past with little more than a passing glance in her direction, if that. She raised her eyes slightly as Allison approached.

"What kind of flowers are you looking for, girl?" the old woman asked. "I have all kinds, for all occasions. High quality, wonderful fragrance." The words were said without enthusiasm, merely memorized and repeated.

"I'm looking for a particular flower," Allison said, holding out the petal. "Could you help me?"

The old woman snorted loudly, then took the petal between two boney fingers. She raised it closer to one eye, closing the other. After a moment of close study, she handed the petal back.

"Royal thane," she said. "Not common. Expensive. You won't find many in this town, and not here."

"Who might be selling these flowers, madam? It's very important."

The old woman said nothing. Her heavy breathing was the only sound heard over the din of customers at Allison's back. Then the old woman reached under the counter of the stall for a piece of paper and a quill pen. She wrote a few curt words on it, then handed it to Allison. The scrawlings appeared to be that of an address.

"Is this a place where they sell this kind of flower?" Allison asked. But the old woman said no more. Allison hesitated for a moment, and got nothing in return but more dull-eyed indifference. Whatever aspect of the conversation had momentarily brought the old woman out of her stupor, had just as quickly gone away again.

Even with the address, finding the location was no easy task. Allison tried asking a few locals, but was met with the same glowering looks as she got from nearly everyone else, despite focusing quite heavily on being polite and nonthreatening. Her persistence did eventually pay off and she was given directions simply to have her go away. The location, a storefront near the eastern edge of town, about a mile north of the King's Crown Inn, was nestled in a copse of other, slightly larger buildings. They were also practically ancient, covered in weathered bricks that had seen a hundred winter storms and held together by mortar brittle enough to crumble at a mere touch.

But the shop was closed. Shuttered, boarded up, and abandoned. It had been that way for a long time. Months, at least, possibly even years. Did no one in Illdara notice when a shop shut down or a business closed its doors? Allison shook her head in disgust, then defiantly planted her hands on her hips. The front door was boarded up, but not as heavily as the match maker's had been.

Allison took out the small knife she kept tucked in her boot and carefully pried up each board. With each nail she pried loose, she counted in her head the number of laws and regulations she was so casually breaking. She promised herself quite vigorously that the boards would be put back into place once she was done.

The musty interior, thick with dust and other floating particles, was just shy of being completely empty. A few loose pieces of decaying furniture stood here and there, where they'd been left after everything else had been taken. The floor was covered in a thin layer of dust, enough to catch the footprints of anyone who happened to walk through, but it bore none save her own.

Allison searched every part of every room, yet found nothing. Anything that might have been considered a clue had long since been carried away, leaving behind just another oddity in a city that seemed full of them. During her search, she'd noticed that the building had a tiny courtyard out back.

It was barely more than twenty feet by twenty feet, and what little space was not taken up by two long structures covered in glass panes-- mostly broken now--was composed of brown, brittle grass. The moist air had simply not been enough to keep the hardy grass alive without hands to care for it. Inside the two structures were rows and rows of wilted flowers. But the flower petal found in the old man's body could not have come from one of those plants, because it had been fresh. Allison lightly touched one of the drooping flowers; its petals and leaves crumbled, pieces falling limply to the floor. Another dead-end.

As she walked back through the building towards the street, her mind wandered and she listened to the tap of her boots against the wood floor. Halfway through the main room, her boot came down and the sound was hollow, different from elsewhere. Allison stood over a thin piece of decorated fabric that had been stretched across the floor.

She pulled it away, but the floor beneath looked little different than anywhere else in the house. Rather than give up, she brushed the dust aside and carefully ran her hands across the floor. Finally, she felt it, an almost imperceptible difference. Her knife slid carefully down into the hairline crack. She pushed it to one side and a section of the floor popped up.

The hole that she stared down into was nearly pitch-black. What little light managed to work it's way down from the house went only a few feet, dimly illuminating a rickety ladder that plunged into that infinite darkness. Allison, always prepared for a variety of eventualities, produced a miniature lantern from a pocket of her frock and lit it with a match. The light from the lantern was no brighter than a small candle and it would only last for a few minutes, but that would have to be enough.

With no more delay, she climbed down the ladder into the basement. The room she found herself in was tiny, far smaller than even the courtyard had been. The light from the lantern stretched from one wall to the other, illuminating everything in between.

Rusted chains dangled from the ceiling in one corner. They bore signs of heavy wear, but as with everything else in the house, had gone unused for quite some time. There were two heavy chairs in another corner, constructed of stout wood and surrounded by a pile of old rags. As the room was otherwise empty, Allison bent down and dug through the pile.

It consisted mostly of strips and sheets of white cloth, soiled and torn, but at the very bottom of the pile, she found a copper ring. It certainly wasn't anything special, merely a plain band of copper. Once it might have been polished to a bright luster, but currently it was covered in ugly, green blotches. Without knowing quite why, Allison stuffed it into one of her pockets.

The room was certainly odd for being the basement of a flower shop, as it felt more like it belonged in a dungeon, but there was little left to give her any clear idea of what the room might have been used for. Of course, but for the decaying greenhouses in the courtyard, there was little evidence left that the building had ever even been a flower shop at all.

As the oil in the lantern was beginning to run out, Allison made one more quick sweep of the basement and, finding nothing more of interest, climbed back up the ladder. The section of floor went back into place and was covered again by the sheet of fabric. Allison stood. Her eyes rose towards the doorway leading to the street. A figure stood there, silhouetted against the gray sky. For a brief instant, the two stared at each other.

Then the figure turned and ran.

Chapter 6

Allison's heart pounded its way up through her throat as she ran after the rapidly-fleeing figure. He was much faster than she was, much more familiar with the streets and alleys as he led her on a merry chase. The people of the city, seemingly so plentiful elsewhere, were now nowhere to be found. It was simply her and her quarry, alone through empty streets and the spidery network of narrow alleys that each took a dozen twisting turns in a dozen different directions.

Far up ahead, the figure burst from the alley, ran across the street, and disappeared through the window of an old factory. Though many of the doors were locked up tight, a single window, which had been broken out at one point, allowed entrance to any with a strong enough desire. Allison stopped at the window and peered inside.

Machinery, covered in dust and rust in equal measure, lay silent and long unused. It was the same story as the flower shop and the match maker. But for today, the building had been without visitor for months, at least, as the lights remained dark and the machinery dead. Allison hoisted herself up through the window and landed on her feet on the other side. Footprints in the dust led deep into the heart of the building, winding around and between presses and cutters and joiners.

Following the footprints wasn't difficult, the pursued had made little attempt to disguise his passage, though he'd had several opportunities to do so. Then suddenly, the tracks stopped. Allison turned one way and then the other, looking for a faint glimpse of movement somewhere within the dark recesses of the cavernous building, or else more footprints to follow. But there were none, she was completely alone.

"You're so close now." The words were a faint whisper, like a breath of air lightly tickling her ears. Allison's hand went to her flintlock pistol. "So close."

"Did you kill those two people?" Allison asked, the words barely making their way up through her throat.

There came no reply. The voice, and whoever it belonged to, was gone. But another sound reached Allison's ears: a faint rustling. She looked up and saw a scrap of paper drifting down from the ceiling. It settled at her feet. The words on it, scrawled with a shaky hand, said "Don't trust the chief inspector, don't trust anyone."

Allison stood for a long time and stared down at the paper. It was ordinary paper and the ink was ordinary ink. The handwriting, as shaky as it was, would provide her with no clues. It had been done that way on purpose, to obfuscate the writer's true hand.

Upon being given this case, she'd suspected that it would be no easy one, that it would feature a long list of complications, and that solving it would take all her powers of deductive reasoning, such as they were. And that there would be no guarantee of coming away with a satisfactory answer. Before, she'd only believed that might be the case. Now, she knew it for the truth.

This man either believed something sinister was afoot or wanted her to believe that was the case in order to hinder her efforts and the efforts of the chief inspector. If no trust existed between them, the case would be that much more difficult to solve. Everything would become tainted by that distrust and the killer would go free.

But if he truly meant what was in the note, and if it were truly of necessity for her to follow its instructions...a shiver ran the length of her spine and not only because the inside of the factory was so very cold. Allison pulled her frock tightly around her chest and did up all the buttons. She crammed the note deep into a pocket, pushing it down beside the copper ring.

Her pocket watch said that it was only two hours past noon, far too early considering how her day had gone. She slipped it back into her frock and then spent the next few hours combing the abandoned factory for any clue that she might have missed.

As the gray sky began to darken, Allison gave up in her search. She'd found nothing, because there simply had been nothing to find. The killer's footprints, leading to a spot near the middle of the building, were all that had been left behind. That, and the note.

As she walked back to the King's Crown Inn, a carriage approached from behind her. It continued on a few dozen feet and then stopped. Inspector Jairyn got out and hurried to her. His face was deeply etched with a fierce scowl, the worst she'd yet seen him with.

"What happened to you?" he demanded. "I thought you were at the coroner's?"

"Something came up," Allison replied, in no mood to get into an argument with him. "I went to track down a lead and that took up most of my day."

The inspector's sigh was awash with exasperation and annoyance. "I've been searching from one side of the city to the other for the entire afternoon, you could at least have told someone where you were going!"

"I didn't have the time for that," Allison said. She jammed her hands deep into the pockets of her frock and started to walk away. After a few steps, she stopped and looked over her shoulder at the inspector. He was still seething. "I came across the killer."

"You *what*?"

"He was waiting when I came out of an abandoned flower shop, which I suspect he purposely led me to. I chased him all the way to an old factory near the docks. He's taunting us, Inspector, and he's no amateur."

The inspector's face flattened until she could no longer read his current emotion. "All the more reason to track him down as quickly as possible and serve him the justice that he's earned for himself. Good day." He got back into the carriage and then, with a whip of the reigns, he and the carriage receded into the distance.

Her clue, her only clue, had led her to an abandoned flower shop, one unused in recent memory, but there the trail stopped. There was also the strange figure to consider. Was he truly the killer? Or was he merely a piece of a larger puzzle, yet waiting to be discovered, much less solved? Allison's mind dwelt more on these things than on her surroundings and so arrived back at the King's Crown almost without realizing it.

The conversations in the tavern were hushed, spoken in little more than whispers. A somber mood had descended upon them, upon the whole city, perhaps, soaking up the light banter and good humor that had been there before. Allison went up to her room and dropped down on the edge of her bed. Although she hadn't noticed it before, she was utterly exhausted. She lay back on the bed and covered her eyes with an arm. So many pieces, so many moving parts, and nothing seemed to fit together as it should.

A knock at her door.

"Yes?"

"Detective?" It was the barmaid from the tavern.

"Come in."

The girl opened the door, revealing a tray of sizzling meat and steaming vegetables, fresh from the kitchen. She set the tray down on a low table.

"You've been working hard today, haven't you?"

Allison nodded, eying the tray of food hungrily.

"I thought you might be, with the way you came in here looking like you'd been run over by a carriage." The girl smiled. "We're all hoping for your success, Detective, even though it doesn't seem that way at times." She bowed her head slightly and then excused herself.

Allison ate all of the food as quickly as she could, suddenly feeling famished. Once the tray was cleared, she set it aside. Her hunger now satiated, she could turn her attention back to the case. Thoughts of sleep were, for the moment, forgotten. She dug around in her pocket and pulled out the note, hoping that she might discover something more that she'd missed earlier.

The copper ring came with the note and slipped beyond her grasp, tinkling faintly as it struck the floor. Allison paused, then put the note away and picked up the ring. Brighter lights revealed nothing that she hadn't already realized about it. It was a small, copper ring, slightly corroded after being left unattended in a damp, dank cellar for an extended amount of time. Nevertheless, there was nothing else that currently needed her attention, so she took it to the wash basin and began to carefully clean it off. Some of the clinging material came away, but most was too attached for water alone.

Allison went down to the kitchen and then came back a few minutes later with a bottle of vinegar and some salt. She mixed the two and then dropped the ring into the solution. She then sat and idly watched as bubbles formed and then drifted slowly to the surface.

At last, Allison had a shiny, copper ring, looking as if it had just come from the jewelers. Only, a jeweler probably wouldn't even sell such a common ring. Allison slowly turned the ring over and over in her hands, looking for any kind of clue or marking that might give her something to work with, however unlikely that might be. Then she saw it, engraved around the inside in tiny letters: *To Julia Ahbin, Beloved.* There were no other markings.

Julia Ahbin...a woman's name. A gift from a husband to a wife, or between two betrothed, perhaps. Yet it was such a cheap gift. A ring like this could be purchased with only a bit more copper than it was made of. And yet the giver had gotten a personal message engraved on it, something which would have cost far more than the ring itself. Curious.

Allison glanced at her watch. A few minutes till five. Time enough to get to police headquarters and search through their archives before sundown, but only just barely. She flipped the ring into the air and then caught in her fist. To police headquarters.

The sky had not yet begun to darken, but the sun was well on its way to the western horizon, occasionally peaking through several layers of thick, gray clouds. The warmth of the day, such as it was, was already giving way to the deadly chill of night. And this particular night was going to be very cold, enough to chill a person's bones if they were out in it. By the look of the clouds, snow was going to start falling before long. Once that happened, the passes would be blocked up until spring came and the temperatures rose. The ships at the harbor were huddled together, as if for warmth. Even the salty water of the bay could not hope to stand against the coming cold for long.

Police headquarters was lightly staffed at such a late hour, as most officers had already gone home and many of the others had just left to begin an evening patrol before the night shift arrived. Allison decided not to bother the chief inspector, at least not yet. At present, she had nothing but a vague hunch. When she knew who this woman was, when she had talked to her or to someone who knew her. Then, she would go to him.

The officer guarding the archives gave her a strange look when she asked to be allowed inside, but did not deter her. He quietly opened the door and then gestured towards the room beyond.

"I'll have to ask that you don't take anything out with you when you leave," was all he said.

The archive was a large room, almost cavernous, and it was filled with dozens of cabinets piled high with documents and records that detailed virtually all information that was worth knowing about Illdara and its residents. There was nothing quite so detailed back in the capital, though it was not so surprising when considering the town's insular nature and relatively small size. Although, given how much the people of Illdara prized their privacy, she wondered whether or not they had any idea that such a storehouse of information existed.

Allison searched out the resident records and began thumbing through stacks until she reached the file for Julia Ahbin. It was brief, with only a few curt lines. Julia Ahbin was twenty-two years old and had lived in Illdara all her life. She'd worked in a tavern for a few months about a year ago. There was no other mention of further employment, either before or since, and she appeared not to have any living relatives. But there was an address, for a tenement out near the edge of the southern arm of the peninsula. Allison committed the information to memory and then replaced the documents. The time was now half past six.

Though she'd felt utterly drained earlier, Allison now felt the thrill that all detectives feel when they're on a case and the next clue, even a tenuous one, is waiting for them to reach out and grasp it. While there were still hours left in the day, she would not sleep.

As Allison walked southeast along Freeman's Way, a wide boulevard that slashed crossways through much of the city, the streets became darker and darker. There were few people out and about, only a handful of workers leaving their jobs as stores and businesses closed or heading to their jobs as taverns and other nocturnal establishments opened. Her presence went largely unnoticed by those she passed, but the ever-present feeling of being watched from somewhere persisted. An itch at the back of her mind that wouldn't go away. Was it real, or imagined? Most foreigners likely felt it regardless.

She checked the address again as she approached Beech Street, which continued west all the way to the cliffs. The southern arm of the city was darker than the rest, meaner and older, with large, blocky buildings pressed so closely together along the narrow streets that they seemed almost to loom outward. Trash was clumped thick in ill-used alleyways where the faint glow of fires emanated from far back in their labyrinthine depths, providing some meager warmth for the homeless and destitute who huddled around them. Less of the order here than elsewhere, but Allison could still feel it.

There were also more eyes here than elsewhere, hidden eyes watching from darkened alleys and darkened windows. The utilitarian cloaks and overcoats of the rest of the city gave way to tattered frocks and soiled coats of thick wool, clothes which had seen many difficult days and gone a long stretch since their last cleaning. Many of the windows that Allison passed were boarded up, either because the inhabitants had left and never returned or from a simple lack of funds to purchase a new window. Heavy, iron bars were set across lower-level windows and doors, as indicative of the nature of the place as anything else she'd seen so far.

A wagon came into view on Allison's right, stopped at the mouth of an alley. Two men were unloading the wagon's cargo as a group of scraggly, desperate-looking men and women stood silently around them. Crates and barrels were opened, food and drink were distributed. Hospitality for the homeless? It was strange to see such a thing in Illdara, though perhaps her opinion of the city was somewhat skewed by being a foreigner. Here, at least, was a good deed being done for those less fortunate. The homeless took the offered food and then quietly returned to their fires deep within the alley. Freeman's gave way to Beech and the wagon passed out of sight.

The apartment where Julia was last known to have lived was at the far end of the street, less than a dozen feet from a sheer cliff. Only a low, rock wall, which hadn't been attended to in a very long time, separated the street from a one hundred foot drop. The crashing of obstinate waves against half-submerged rocks was an ever-present thing, as steady and as reliable as the slow beat of a funeral march.

Allison walked up to the front door, reached through the iron bars, and knocked several times. The sound was like thunder in the still, night air.

The building was old and silent, filled with dark windows whose curtains and shutters were drawn tight. No candles burned in any of those windows, she saw nothing at all to indicate that the building was occupied by any save the old ghosts of the past. Even the address plate near the door was rusty, the once-lustrous copper turned a sickly green so that the numbers were barely legible.

The latch on the door *clicked* and the door slid open a fraction of an inch. The darkness was too deep to see anything of the one who'd opened it.

"Yes?" came a whispered question.

"I'm looking for someone," Allison said. "Julia Ahbin."

"No one here by that name."

"According to public records, this is her last known place of residence. If I could just-"

But before Allison could say more, the door was slammed firmly shut and a sturdy bolt slid into place. Knocking on the door a second time would gain her little, so she made a slow circuit of the building.

Gaining entrance through a back door or lower window was impossible, as the thick, metal bars across both would stop only the most practiced lock-pick or someone of considerable strength, neither of which Allison could express to being. As she walked back to the front of the building, a window above her slid open.

"Hey, you," someone whispered down to her.

Allison stopped and looked up at the window, but saw nothing save darkness.

"Garrison Park, one hour."

The window slid closed again.

Allison stared up at the window for a long time. Her mind ran through a myriad of potential outcomes, mulling over clues and hints, wondering, in the depth of Illdara's bitterly-cold, winter night, as large flakes of snow were even now beginning to fall, if going to Garrison Park was really such a good idea.

Chapter 7

One hour was all it took for the ground to be covered in a thin layer of white powder. Allison's thick frock was little barrier against the cold wind that blew off the sea and whipped the flakes across the ground. An hour ago, it hadn't been so bad. But the intervening time had made the situation decidedly unbearable and Allison pined for her bed at the King's Crown as she stood beneath a flickering, gas flame.

Garrison Park, much like its name suggested, was home to a number of military trinkets and mementos. The turret from an old fort that had stood at the mouth of the harbor for centuries, a few rusted cannons, and several statues of heroes and leaders that lived on only as faded legends with less truth than an old salt's oft-repeated fishing stories. A smattering of trees, all long dead, intertwined with winding, gravel paths.

Ahead of her, in the near-blinding snow and darkness, a figure appeared, hood pulled down low over the face.

"You came," the figure said. Allison had half-expected another run-in with the murderer, but the voice this time was different, younger and with a higher pitch.

"Why couldn't you have met me somewhere else?" Allison asked. "Somewhere warmer?"

The figure looked left, then right. "No one will be here at night," he said, "this is the only place we could meet without being seen or heard."

Allison's visible breath appeared and was quickly drawn away by the wind. The night was only going to get colder and the snow thicker. "Alright, say what you've come here to say, then."

"You're looking for Julia, aren't you? I heard you speaking to Ms. Lurin, the landlady. She...Julia was everything to me! Everything!"

Allison took the ring from her pocket and held it up. "*You* gave this to her?"

The figure nodded slowly, his eyes fixed on the glimmering ring. "I did, more than a year ago. Feels like an eternity." His hand rose as if unconsciously reaching for the ring, even though it was much too far away. Then he seemed to realize what he was doing and lowered his hand. "She deserved much better than that, much better. A diamond, at least. But how could I afford that?" A choking sob, barely held back.

"What happened to her?" Allison asked. "Why was her ring in the basement of that old flower shop?"

The young man began to nervously wring his hands, his hood twisting this way and that. They were alone in the park, completely alone. Allison took a step towards him.

"No!" he exclaimed. "Don't come any closer!" He took a step back and nearly fell. "They can't know I've been here, they can't. Do you understand? Maybe...maybe they already know, we've been here for so long!"

He was raving, his eyes wild and savage like a cornered beast. Whatever he might know, he was the beyond the point of being able to properly explain it. Allison found herself at a loss, unsure of what to say or do. The young man paused in his fidgeting, his eyes fixed on her. Without warning, he ran forward, grabbing Allison by the shoulders before she could reach for her pistol and nearly pushing her to the ground.

"They came in the night!" he exclaimed. "Dark cloaks, dark faces! Always the same when they come! Always the same!" The hood of his cloak slipped off his head, revealing a face that was etched with scars and smudged with grime. He must have seen the shock in her eyes, because he let go of her and stepped away. "When I awoke, she was gone. The shadows took her, like they take everyone. Soon they'll be nothing left but empty streets and empty buildings. Empty, dead." His eyes grew wide, white all around the irises. "They took her into the deep places, took her for their...their..."

A strong gust of wind sprayed snow in Allison's face and she raised her hand to ward it off. When it stopped, and she lowered her arm, the young man was gone. The erratic marks of his boots as they fled into the darkness were already disappearing.

Her hands shook and not just from the cold. The King's Crown Inn was no short distance away and she desperately wanted to be back there, now more than ever. Allison pulled her frock more tightly around herself and walked back along Freeman's Way towards Highmark Street, trying to make some sense of what she'd witnessed. And looking often over her shoulder.

The wind died down after a time and the snow stopped falling quite so hard, though the night was still bitterly cold. The road through the mountains was likely already impassible and it wouldn't be long before the harbor froze over, sealing everyone and everything inside Illdara's cold, unfriendly grasp. The bell tower tolled ten o'clock.

A few blocks from Highmark Street, Allison heard the dull echo of boots in the distance. Without thinking, she ducked into a narrow alley and waited. After a few moments, figures appeared from out of the darkness. They wore dark cloaks with hoods pulled low. Silvery masks shimmered in the light of their lanterns and long, slender swords bounced and swayed at their hips. One in front carried a tall pole with a strange symbol fixed atop it. Twenty, perhaps, possibly a bit more. Allison held her breath as they marched slowly past.

She was tired, more than tired, and the night air was so very cold. More than anything else, she wanted to be safely tucked into her bed at the inn, where she wouldn't have to think about murders and murderers, secrets meetings in the night, and the suspicious glower of everyone who lived in this forsaken city. She wanted to be back home at the capital, desperately so.

Yet she followed them. They marched up Main Street, past city hall and the Fountain Square, where the great fountain still strained against the encroaching chill, all the way to Barrister Road. They turned right, following the cliffs along the northern edge of the city. The procession continued to the lighthouse at the end of the street, as if drawn there inexorably by some powerful, unseen force. They slowly disappeared through an opening just to the right of the main door, down several steps. Then the metal doors were shut tight as the last of them went through. The light at the top of the lighthouse continued to slowly turn and the only sound left in the world was the clanging and groaning of its rusting gears.

The bell tower tolled midnight just before Allison found herself back at the King's Crown Inn. The bright lights that shown through the windows and around the edges of the front door were a welcome beacon after so long a day and so long a night. Even from without, she could hear the muted carousing that went on inside those stout walls. The murder of earlier in the day had been forgotten amidst the flow of ale and other hard drinks. It might be somber again in the morning, but for a little while, they could live once more.

Allison slid slowly past filled tables, still packed with locals and travelers alike nearly an hour past midnight. Among that rowdy lot were a few sailors, those more adventurous than their fellows; a couple of merchants, staying the winter in Illdara to oversee some business deal or another; and those locals who were a bit more keen on mingling with outsiders than the rest. With the cold chill of winter finally settling in after days of blustery threats, they'd likely not leave even when the sun rose again. The drinking would go on into the night and those who could afford to do so would sleep away much of the day on the coin they'd managed to save through the toil of spring, summer, and autumn.

A dozen different conversations all rattled away simultaneously, but Allison did not hear any of what was being said. She was tired, so tired that she could hardly think straight anymore. Her fingers, toes, and face all felt as if they'd frozen into a solid block of ice, stinging and burning. A small comfort, in a way, as it indicated that she'd not stayed out long enough to catch frostbite.

"Have you not slept at all, Detective?" the barmaid asked. Allison realized that she still did not know the girl's name. When Allison shook her head, the girl clicked her tongue. "That's no good, no good at all." She wordlessly took Allison's frock and then guided her toward a back room. "We've got some water fresh from over the fire, as I thought you might need it when you finally returned. You ought to take better care of yourself, you know? If you looked run over by a carriage before, you look twice that now."

Allison did not resist as the girl gently pushed her into a small room at the back of the tavern, behind the kitchen, where half of a large barrel was filled with clear, steaming water. Nor even when the girl pealed off the rest of her sweat-and-snow-logged clothes and took them away. Allison was soon left alone, standing stark naked in the middle of the tiny room.

She hoisted herself up over the lip of the barrel and slid down into the water. A sharp pain, like prodding needles, surged along her arms and legs as goosebumps popped up on her skin. The water was hot enough, and her body cold enough, that the pain was almost unbearable. But soon the pain faded and the warmth of the water soothed tired muscles and aching joints. She almost fell asleep.

The girl came back a little while later, clean clothes in hand. She'd done a very good job of cleaning and drying the clothes in such a short time. Allison mumbled her thanks as the girl set the clothes to one side, until they were needed again.

"Marcia Loren," the girl said, smiling. At Allison's confused expression, she added, "I remembered that I hadn't even told you my name yet."

"Allison Newberry, though I imagine you know that already."

"I did overhear it, yes," Marcia said. She brought out several large towels from a chest at the back of the room and held them up. Allison pulled herself out of the water, despite the protest of nearly every muscle in her body, and wrapped herself in one of the towels and used another to dry her arms and legs.

"Your work must be awfully difficult, to keep you out all day and all night."

"I can't say too much," Allison said, "but I suspect there is much more work yet to be done before this is all over."

There was something else the girl wanted to say, but she held her tongue and stared down at the floor. Her hands worked nervously and her eyes betrayed a conflict of emotions.

"You can tell me anything you like," Allison said, "I'll not pass it along to anyone else, if you want, not even to Inspector Jairyn."

At this, the girl raised her head. "It's just...no one will say so, Ms. Newberry, but they're all afraid, thinking that this killer might strike again. Nobody's safe from him, they say. If he'll kill a politician's wife and even stoop to killing an old beggar, who won't he come after? People say...they say he's a foreigner, might have even come here on one of the ships. They talk like maybe it wouldn't be so bad if all the outsiders were rounded up. Here's not so bad, but I heard that in other places there...there have been incidents."

"Incidents?"

"A couple of sailors got drunk and started talking, a group of men ambushed them later in an alley and beat them up pretty badly. That's the worst one, I suppose, but a lot of angry words have been thrown around today. Everybody was talking about it earlier, before it got dark and they started drinking."

"Then what you're saying is," Allison said slowly, "if this continues on much longer, and if more people fall prey to the killer, the situation is likely to get much worse?"

Marcia nodded her head, unable to even speak the words. They were all trapped in the city. With the snow beginning to fall, the pass through the mountains was blocked. Even travel by sea wouldn't be possible, as the frozen spray from the wind-tossed waves would quickly gather on every surface, weighing ships down and capsizing them if they ventured too far from the docks. And after a few more weeks, the harbor itself would be frozen over. Nowhere was left for the outsiders in the city to go. If the people worked themselves up enough, even the police would not be able to stop them. If the killings continued, the tension *would* boil over. Not if...*when*.

"Thank you for telling me," Allison said quietly.

She threw the towels aside and dressed in her own clothes again. It felt good to wear clean clothes after days on the road and then being too busy since to even bother changing. The fabric was soft against her skin and the faint smell of flowers, replacing the stench of stale sweat, was a welcome change.

She was left with a lot to think about, a lot to wonder about, and a lot to try to find out about. With her head feeling as if it was stuffed full of cotton and her eyelids feeling as heavy as iron shutters, she simply could not properly focus on any of those things. She thanked Marcia for the bath, and the information, and went up to her room. Candle light shown under the door to Martin's room and Allison considered knocking, but decided against it. His thoughts would have to wait, at least until after a good, long sleep.

Fresh blankets, and a few more than the night before, had been brought to her room and were piled high on her bed. A lone candle was burning on the nightstand. The air was cold, but Allison cast off most of her clothes anyway and then quickly climbed under the blankets, before pulling them up to her chin. She rolled over and blew out the candle.

The silent darkness of her room was so very welcoming. She could push aside all other thoughts and listen to the rhythmic pounding of her heart, the rush of blood through her veins, as her consciousness slowly faded. And that was exactly what she did.

Morning came slowly, sluggishly, for Allison. Her pocket watch said that it was nearly three hours past sunrise, but hardly any light came in around the shutters on her window. Braving the chill air, she got up and threw them back.

The sky outside was dark, filled with black clouds as thick as the crowd in the capital's main market on King's Day. Outside, it was almost as dark as night and the snow was still falling. Ice hung in thick spikes from the roof above the window, waiting to pop loose and crash down onto some unsuspecting pedestrian's head. Such a thing was not entirely uncommon.

Allison wondered why she was thinking about that. Most likely it was tied to the fact that she still felt the previous day and night acutely in most of her joints and because her mind was still not fully awake, preferring to draw upon random threads rather than anything coherent or relevant.

She stumbled her way down the stairs to the common room, which, even well into the morning, was still full of customers. Some were working on curing their overnight hangover by drinking even more of the stuff that had put them in that situation to begin with. At a table near the back, Allison spotted Martin. He was sipping from a tall stein, although the fact that steam curled upward through the opening suggested that he was not drinking an alcoholic beverage, and staring intently at several yellowed documents. Allison sat down across from him.

"You were up late last night, Mr. Roundtree," Allison said.

"And you, as well, love, if you knew that *I* was up so late," he quipped, setting aside the documents.

"Detectives rarely keep regular hours."

Martin smiled at that. "Aye, nor does the bookkeeper of a major merchant house, even when all roads into town are closed for the winter." He sipped from his stein, which Allison saw was filled with coffee. "So, how goes the investigation, Detective?"

"Not so well," Allison said, being honest. "I've spent the past few days running from one side of the city to the other and I've got more unanswered questions now than when I started."

Martin nodded knowingly. "Things are rarely ever easy or simple in Illdara, anyone who's ever been here before can tell you that. Well, I've faith in you, Detective, that you'll soon have that fellow who's been running around stabbing people to death put behind bars."

Allison tapped his stein with the back of her hand. "I'll drink to that."

Martin laughed, pausing only to drink deeply of his coffee.

"Of course," Allison said, "that's assuming I live long enough to catch up to him."

"Oh?"

72

Allison dropped her voice. "The girl who works here has heard some stories that don't leave me with a great deal of confidence in that. Apparently, outsiders are regarded even less than usual these days, to the point where the townsfolk might start becoming openly hostile if this goes on much longer."

"Hmm..." said Martin, appearing a bit troubled at the news. "I'd not heard of that. It's...certainly something to think on."

Marcia soon brought around a plate of food and another tall stein full of steaming coffee, which Allison made quick work of. Her head had finally begun to clear by then and she took a mental stock of everything that would need her attention. There was the strange cult, or whatever they might be, she'd seen disappear beneath the lighthouse and the disappearance of Julia Ahbin under circumstances that her boyfriend, an unhinged, untrustworthy young man, deemed malicious. It was possible that the two were, in some way, connected, but it was a stretch with what little evidence she had, which was just a fraction more than none at all. And there was still the culprit to contend with, along with the unrest being stirred up by his actions.

Allison stood. "We'll speak more another time, perhaps. Until then."

Martin lifted his stein and tipped his head slightly. "So long, love, knock 'em dead out there."

Whether from the snow, at several inches deep and still falling, or the general sense of anxiousness that was blanketing the city, the streets were mostly empty. Those few who ventured out were quick to arrive at their destination and quick to return home. Even the stalls in the market on Highmark Street--most of them, anyway--were boarded up and empty.

Only the most intrepid, or desperate, merchants were trying to hawk their wares, and having little luck at it.

The muted sounds of the city, almost muted to silence, gave Allison an odd feeling, of being in some otherworldly place. The capital was not immune to snow storms, but even then the streets were filled with the pounding of boots and horses' hooves as the city continued in its routines, tamping down the blanket of snow until the streets were easily passable. Not so in Illdara. When the snow fell, the city ground to a halt. But the snow might only be an excuse this winter.

Police headquarters was crowded with officers, who had taken to working at their desks rather than walking their beats. A lamp was burning brightly in Inspector Jairyn's office, so she quietly let herself in. The noisy babble from the main room became muted, distant.

"Have you something worthy of my time, Detective Newberry?" he asked, in a tone that suggested he was only being as polite as he was at present through sheer force of will.

"I've nothing truly worth even *my* time, Inspector," she told him, "but I would rather spend that time on these things than on nothing at all."

"Fine," he said flatly. "Ask such questions as you like and then be on your way, I am not so fortunate as you to be unburdened by important affairs."

"So it would seem," Allison mumbled. Louder, she said, "What can you tell me of the state of religious affairs here in Illdara?"

One of the inspector's eyebrows rose slightly. "The local Temple is the central institution," he said, "the same as back in the capital."

"On the surface, perhaps, but are you sure there are no splinter groups? Robed men and women who stalk the streets in the dead of night and perform secret rituals below the lighthouse?"

Jairyn leaned back, his face pensive. "You'd find out soon enough with that much information in hand, so there's little reason not to tell you. Those you refer to are the Duganites, worshipers of some pagan god or another. I've dealt with them before, but as they keep mostly to themselves, they are allowed to carry out such practices as they desire. So long as they are not a bother to anyone and refrain from breaking any of the city's laws, I have no cause to intrude myself into their business."

"Has there been any trouble with them in the past?" Allison asked.

"Trouble? Not in so many words," Jayrin replied. "The Temple priests have lodged a few complaints, most of which were deemed to have little basis in fact. You can read their file, if you like, but I'll warrant you won't find any more than I've already told you."

Allison briefly considered pressing the issue, and raising the disappearance of Julia Ahbin, but decided against it. She was already, clearly, trying the chief inspector's patience and so excused herself. A trip to the archives proved what he'd told her: the file for the Duganite cult was a small one and contained little in the way of their beliefs or practices, or even any names to look up. She did find, however, in another file, the name of the man who owned and operated the lighthouse: a Mr. Giles Elder.

A long walk up Cedar and along Barrister, pushing through snow piled up to her knees in some places. Nearly seven miles, but it felt like three times that. The fountain at Fountain Square was frozen solid, as if time, for it, had stopped during the night. She saw more empty streets, with the only signs of life coming from the fires that burned deep within the city's labyrinth of alleys. The homeless had no choice but to stay out in the bone-chilling air.

High up on the lighthouse, Allison saw a light burning in a window, a single candle. She pounded loudly on the door at its base with a gloved hand. After several moments, the door creaked open a few inches, showing an eye, but little else.

"I'm looking for the master of this lighthouse," she said, "Giles Elder."

The door opened a bit wider, showing the whole man. He was old, bordering on ancient, with a back that bent forward and eyes that were a milky-blue. The records had suggested that he'd owned the lighthouse for a very long time.

"You're looking at him," the old man said. "What business you got here, girl?"

"I was hoping to ask you a few questions, specifically about the Duganites."

The old man frowned at the mention of the cult. "Got nothing to say about them," he said, "certainly not to you. There anything else you'd care to pester me about?"

Cold air and flakes of drifting snow were carried in through the open door by the same wind that tugged at the fringes of Allison's frock.

"Perhaps I could pester you more inside, where it's not quite so cold?"

The old man's frown deepened and Allison half-expected him to slam the door in her face. To her surprise, he pulled the door open a bit further. Allison ducked as she entered, just barely missing the head jamb. The door was firmly shut behind her.

The round room on the bottom floor of the lighthouse was lit by a cheery fire consisting of several large, cedar logs, crackling and popping in a very inviting manner. Two high-backed chairs were set in front of it, on top of a thick rug of many eye-catching patterns and colors. Something was sizzling in a wide pan on top of a pot-bellied stove. The windows on the bottom floor were all covered with thick curtains.

"Didn't think I'd have guests," Giles said, "didn't put on enough for anybody else."

"That's perfectly fine, Mr. Elder, I ate just recently."

The old man grunted as he attended to his lunch. Allison went to an empty chair and sat, extending her frozen hands toward the fire.

"It must be lonely, living all the way out on the northern arm in this old lighthouse."

Giles grunted a second time as he moved a few sizzling pieces of meat from the pan to a small plate. "Don't nobody bother me up here, least that's what I thought until today."

"What about the Duganites, do they not bother you?"

"Far as I'm concerned, they can do as they like, so long as they come after I go to sleep and don't stir up a racket. Unlike you, they don't come around during the day where decent folks have to see what it is they're up to."

"You're not the least bit curious?" Allison asked.

"Ain't nobody in Illdara *curious*, girl, that ain't our way," the old man said angrily, pointing an accusing finger at her. "You let me keep to my business and I'll let you keep to yours. Bad enough we gotta deal with foreigners, now we got *nosy* foreigners."

"Unfortunately, Mr. Elder, it's my job to be nosy, otherwise a man who's already killed two people, and may very well kill again, will go free. You know as well as I do that the people of Illdara, curious or not, would like to see this matter over and done with."

"Foreign influence," Giles grunted. He sat down at a small table and began to eat. "Didn't used to have killings and thefts and whatnot before they started letting all those ships into the harbor," he said in between bites, "bringing suspicious types with 'em. You mark me, girl, the one what's doing the killing ain't from Illdara. Came on a ship'd be my guess. You mark me on that."

"Well, it wasn't the nature of the killer that brought me here today, what I'd really like to know about is the cult. Specifically, what sorts of things they believe and what their practices are."

"None of the Duganites ever killed anybody," Giles insisted.

"Whether they did or didn't, I'd like to know just the same."

"Nothing to tell. If you're in it, you know; if you're not, you don't. Simple as that."

"And what must one do to get into the cult?"

Giles glanced at her out of the corner of his eyes. She was clearly trying what little patience he had. "Why don't you ask them yourself?"

"I would, if I knew whom to ask."

Giles stared at her a moment longer, then rose and found a sheet of loose paper. He wrote a few things on it with a quill pen and then handed it to her. *Main and Beech, Faustus Prin*, said the note.

"He'll tell you, if it pleases him to."

"Thank you, Mr. Elder," Allison said. "Have you lived in Illdara long?"

"Long enough," he said. Giles rose and took his empty plate to the sink, where he began to scrub away any clinging food with a bit of water.

"Long enough for what?"

But the old man said nothing.

Allison stood after a few moments. "And there's really nothing else you can tell me?"

"Not to you, or anyone," Giles said, his back still turned to her.

"Good day, then."

Chapter 8

Well into the afternoon, beneath a sky still hidden behind thick, gray clouds and amidst the swirl of errant snow, Allison finally arrived at the address to which she'd been directed by Giles Elder.

The building was a very old one, but well taken care of. Behind a high, stone wall and an iron gate, behind tall columns adorned from feet to crown with clinging ivy, was a wide building, far wider than deep, that stood between Beech Street and the cliffs that dropped down to the sea. Large windows with dark-purple curtains, pulled tight, were evenly placed on both floors of the building. The front doors were made of thick, dark wood, looking both heavy and imposing. A tall dome, perfectly circular, capped off the roof in the exact center of the building. It was not far removed from the houses commonly owned by nobles back at the capital.

Allison entered the grounds through the gate, which was unlocked, and walked up to the doors. A wide variety of aquatic animals had been carved into the wood and the polished, brass knockers were suspended from the mouths of twin sea serpents of some kind. She reached up and knocked loudly on the left door.

After a few moments, the door opened, allowing Allison to view a well-lit interior and the well-dressed man who stood in it. He looked to be in his late-thirties and was moderately handsome, with a trimmed mustache and dark hair parted halfway from his left ear to the top of his head. He even dressed the part of a noble. With one hand to his breast, he bowed deeply.

"We thought you might come here soon enough, merely a matter of talking to the right people."

He stepped through the doorway and then shut the door behind him. Then he extended a hand towards the street. "We will walk as we talk, if you do not mind. The past few days have kept me inside and I feel the brisk air shall do me some good."

Allison did mind, having spent most of the day walking those snow-clogged streets, but didn't want to upset someone who might potentially be a source of information.

"You're Faustus Prin, I take it?" Allison asked as they walked west on Beech Street.

"One and the same," the man replied. "From whom did you come by my name?"

"Giles Elder, at the lighthouse."

"Ah, you followed us there, did you? You are of a curious sort."

"Curiosity is a necessary trait in a detective," Allison said.

Faustus laughed lightly. "True enough, though it's a trait not well looked upon here. I'm surprised that Giles did not throw you out when you started questioning him. A man who lives in the most isolated part of the most isolated city in the world likely has a reason for such a life."

"I appealed to his good nature," Allison said blandly. "You're a difficult man to find, if you don't mind me saying so, it took some work to discover your particular religion and that you were its head."

"That is how we like things to be here in Illdara," Faustus said. "And it took me no small amount of money and influence to keep my name from being plastered across every other report in Inspector Jairyn's archive. He is a man who understands the value of information, do not think otherwise."

"Now, if you do not mind," Allison said, "I'd like to ask you a few questions."

"If I was not of a mind to assuage your curiosity, I'd have left you at the doorstep."

Icy spray from the waves that crashed against the cliffs drifted up to the city and swirled around them on the wind, making the street a poor place to hold a conversation. Faustus Prin seemed open and polite enough, given how most in the city reacted to her presence, but Allison had been around enough people to know that he was not answering her questions as a personal favor to her. Beyond that...well, who knows?

"I'd like to know about your order, Mr. Prin," Allison said, "what you believe and what practices you take part in."

"Our beliefs are a reaction to the Temple and its arrogance," he said. "If you are a religious woman, then I apologize for my bluntness, but we believe that the Temple has become too focused on the material world, the accumulation of wealth and the construction of grand buildings, they have forgotten what it truly means to worship an entity with the power to determine our fate and the fate of the world."

"You seem to have an affinity for the sea," Allison noted.

"True enough, the sea is the mother of all things, the origin of life, and the sea is our lifeblood. There are no fields for tilling or for raising animals for the slaughter, there is only the sea and it's great bounty. If the sea rages, the sailor suffers. If the sea is calm, the sailor draws in his reward. Our lives are not so secure that we are afforded the luxury of a pantheon of gods and goddesses, to worship at our leisure. There is the sea and there is Illdara. Nothing more."

"And if someone happened to share your beliefs, what would they need to do in order to join? Or if someone joined and then had second thoughts?"

Faustus smiled again, just a faint twisting of the edges of his lips, but it seemed not to reach the rest of his face. "To join, one must simply come to us and ask entrance. If they've true faith, it shall be shortly revealed. To leave...well, we certainly hope that they would not, but how could we force someone to continue practicing a false faith?"

"Does the name 'Julia Ahbin' mean anything to you?" Allison finally asked.

Faustus stopped. "I am...not intimately familiar with every single member of our order. That privilege is left to those more suited to such things than I." That faint smile never faded. "If she is among our order, then you must ask her yourself. Privacy, Detective, is Illdara's great treasure, and we prize it more than others."

Far behind them, a coach appeared from out of the swirling snow, drawn by a pair of very large horses. Once it had come to a stop beside them, Faustus politely dipped his head and then opened the door to the coach.

"I'm afraid I must leave you here, good detective," he said. "Until we meet again."

The door was shut, the coach continued on and disappeared back into the swirling snow. Allison was left alone, standing in the middle of a street piled high with snow that was finally beginning to melt under the meager warmth from the sun. Not enough to make an appreciable difference, but enough for it to soak into her frock and boots and much of the rest of her clothes. The King's Crown Inn was nearly two miles away.

What now? The thought reverberated through her head. The old man at the lighthouse didn't know anything. If Faustus Prin knew anything, he wasn't going to say so, and they'd not just let her inside to dig through their archives. Julia Ahbin's boyfriend was too lost in his own madness to provide any more information than he already had. There was no one left to ask, no clues left to investigate. *What now?*

Her watch showed that it was past three o'clock, still plenty of daylight left to do the things that all detectives did when there was a murderer on the loose. If not for the feeling that a cold was already well on its way, she might have just stalked the streets for another few hours, hassling anyone that she could run down. As it was, she started back to the inn.

After turning onto Freeman's, she stared idly at the faint glow of a fire from deep within an alley, pulsing against the faceless, windowless walls of the buildings all around. A thought occurred to her and she wondered why she'd not thought of it before. It was such a simple thing, but of course, implausible. It was for that reason that it came to her when she had no other threads to cling to. The homeless saw things, knew things, that others were more likely to miss. And they might just be a bit more inclined to talk, particularly if a bit of money came their way.

The mud and dirt and refuse of the alley was hidden beneath a thick layer of snow, piled higher in some places than out in the street. The radiant heat from the fire was doing it's best to melt away some of the snow, especially as she pressed deeper into the alley, but the cold air and the cold winds were doing their best to keep the snow frozen.

After a few moments, she reached an open area where several alleys met. A fire burned brightly amidst a gathering of ragged tents and rotting crates that served as shelters. They were all empty, even the makeshift seats around the fire were unoccupied. There was not a soul around, living or otherwise. Had they died from the cold and snow, their bodies would still be around. To make no mention of their fire, which would not last long unattended.

With care, Allison searched the places where the homeless slept, curled up beneath moth-eaten blankets and other discarded bits of cloth. She found little in the way of personal affects, though that was hardly surprising. The snow around the encampment came next, but it was undisturbed, totally without footprints save her own.

Curious. No...strange. It was as if the people there, and surely people had been there and not so long ago, had simply vanished into the air, drawn away by the wind like a vapor.

Something was odd about the fire. At first, Allison could not figure out just what it was that did not sit right in her mind as she stared at those flames. But as she stared deeper, a realization came. Several logs were in the midst of the fire, big logs that would keep a good fire going for some time, but it did not appear as though the logs were actually ablaze themselves.

She carefully kicked one of the logs out of the fire. It rolled, smoking, across the cobblestones as the snow it touched hissed and sizzled. No fire was coming off of it. The fire in front of her continued to burn just as strong as before. Allison inspected the log and found it not to be wood at all, but a carved bit of stone, hollow in the middle. Now even "strange" wasn't quite enough.

She'd seen the homeless here in Illdara before, huddled before their fires, she *had* seen them, it wasn't merely her imagination. This was the same alley to which she'd seen a wagon delivering food just the day before. Yet what explanation could there be for what she saw? With her curiosity at it's peak, Allison searched the surrounding buildings, digging away layers of snow and ice, digging down to the cobblestones, looking for some clue, some indication, that might provide an answer that could possibly explain what this all meant.

Finally, her efforts paid off. Hidden in a remote corner of the area where the alleys converged, underneath a pile of rubbish and other foul-smelling things, she found a large metal disc set into the cobblestones. Such things had been used back in the capital to allow entrance to the city's sewer system, and likely it served a similar purpose here. Allison was still completely alone, and there weren't even any windows looking down on her in this unfriendly alley. She pried up one side of the disc with a small knife and hoisted it out of the way.

A round tube, descending into the ground, into a dark chasm, yawned back at her. Rusted, iron rungs were set into the stone, but it was hard to tell whether they'd been used recently. She'd not thought to bring a lantern with her this time.

Allison slammed her first against the wall. The pain did little to dull her annoyance with herself. Without a light, she would have to be insane to venture down into those dark depths. Insane or desperate and she was not that desperate. Not yet.

Her discovery, and all the possible things it might mean, were carefully filed alongside all the other oddities she'd come across since first arriving in Illdara. That list was not a small one and it appeared to be growing with each passing day. Allison also realized that her cold was getting worse.

The mysterious tunnel, and what secrets it might hide, would have to wait for another day. Unfortunately, that day was not to come anytime soon.

Chapter 9

It snowed that night. And snowed, and snowed, and snowed. The snow didn't let up until late in the evening of the next day, by which time it had climbed up above the first floor windows. Everyone inside the tavern was, for all intents and purposes, trapped. Marcia assured Allison that the inn's larder was well-stocked, with enough food for all the patrons and guests to eat and drink comfortably for some time, although she did not specify exactly how long "some time" was.

Allison sipped from a steaming mug and looked out over the white expanse. Great chunks of ice drifted on the slowly undulating sea, gathering in the harbor around the ships as errant bergs drifted down from the icepack still waiting in the north. It would not have much longer to do so.

It wasn't that she had an abundance of leads to check out, because she didn't, but the idea of being trapped in the inn, while the killer remained at large and while so many questions that desperately needed answers remained unanswered, was more than she could bear. She sat and stared out the window, sipping occasionally from the mug, watching as the city lay silently sleeping beneath its thick blanket.

When the mug was empty, she slammed it down on the table, as much annoyed with the weather as anything else. At the very least, it most likely meant that the killer was trapped inside somewhere, as well. And there'd at least not be any riots or round-ups of outsiders until the snow cleared. Though who knew when that would be?

Having exhausted the entertainment she derived from the view, Allison picked up the mug and took it downstairs with her. The mood in the common room in no way suggested that everyone was trapped inside nor did it have any of the gloomy, hushed conversations she'd heard after the second murder. All worries and all cares were casually thrown aside, all responsibilities forgotten, as long as the snow stayed. They were free to eat and drink as they pleased. Given that snow of this magnitude was a common occurrence in Illdara's winter months, they'd likely saved all year just for such an occasion.

She listened halfheartedly to their conversations, but heard only wild tales from days gone by, gossip of this person or that, and so on. Half of what she heard was grossly exaggerated, the other half being an outright lie. The curiosity that was absent in the rest of the city was still alive and well at the King's Crown Inn, at least. Unfortunately, no one gossiped about their neighbors being cold-blooded killers or having secret information about the Duganite cult or why some of the city's homeless seemed to have vanished. It would be nice to come across someone who'd give her straight, informative answers for once, but it was unlikely she'd find such a thing from a group of boisterous men and women downing tall steins of local alcohol as if they were working on the last batch ever to be brewed.

Martin, if he was still at the inn, had not made an appearance and Marcia was too busy to stop and chat, so Allison picked the least crowded table she could find in the most secluded corner of the common room and drank more of the inn's coffee, a stout brew made from beans a thousand leagues from home. Allison was as far from the windows at the front of the building as she could get, but still eyed them warily whenever she heard the wood creak or groan against the massive weight of all that snow. They weren't likely to cave in, spilling tons of snow all over the inn's patrons, but that gnawing fear remained.

Allison spent much of the day sitting at the table and running through every clue she could remember, trying to somehow make each piece fit together with the others. Her luck in that regard was limited. Too many of the pieces had odd edges or strange patterns, nothing that seemed similar to any other piece. Surely there existed, somewhere, a piece that they would all attach to. Thinking about the clues over and over only made her head hurt worse than it already was from a mild cold.

It did not snow again after that first day, but the snow that had already fallen lingered. Even when the sun finally made its appearance, seemingly the first appearance it'd made since her arrival, the snow persisted. It clung to roofs and streets alike, intent on staying put, seemingly, until the warm, southerly winds of spring finally drove it away.

One day passed and Allison prowled the halls of the inn, pacing back and forth. Two days passed and Allison spent her time lying on her bed, staring up at the ceiling. Three days passed and Allison didn't bother getting up until well after midday and went back to sleep after only a few hours. Four days passed and Allison went back to pacing the halls, her hands and feet itching and her mind racing. Five days passed.

The same view of white from the window, the harbor becoming more and more frozen with each passing day, the monotony of the same stories told in the common room, the same people, the same rooms. They slowly chiseled away at Allison's sanity until she was prepared to hop out of a second story window and take her chances.

"You really ought to calm down, Detective," Marcia said, not failing to notice the obvious warning signs of cabin fever.

"I can't stand this," Allison said, her voice low, dangerously unhinged. "I can't bear to sit around for days on end, powerless to do anything!"

"There's nothing you can do about the weather, it's just gonna do what it wants. Now, just yesterday I saw that some of the snow was melting away, I'm sure by tomorrow or the day after you'll be able to go back outside and continue your investigation." She raised her head and looked towards the stairs. "Here comes that nice Mr. Roundtree you spoke about before." She waved one of her hands in his direction and nodded. "Haven't seen him in nearly a week and I bet you haven't either. Why don't you strike up a nice conversation with him and forget about all that snow."

Allison sighed, realizing that it was fruitless to argue with the girl once she got a thought in her head. Martin slowly descended the staircase, his eyes bloodshot and his hair disheveled. He approached Allison's table and then carefully eased himself into an empty chair, before lowering his face into his hands.

"Bloody weather," he mumbled.

"And I thought all this snow was hard on *me*," Allison said.

Martin raised his eyes, but a stein of coffee was slid under his nose before he could make his remark. He drank the brew in several painful gulps and then sighed loudly as he set the stein back down.

"I've had nothing to do for the past five days," he said, "but to stare at the same stack of shipping manifests and cargo logs over and over and I still can't make proper sense of them. If it weren't my skin on the line, I'd have burned the whole lot of them days ago."

"Poor Martin, it must be so hard on you."

"Aye, love, life in the employ of a wealthy merchant is naught but hardship and toil, with nary a word of thanks when the day ends." If he picked up on her sarcasm, he certainly didn't show it.

"Marcia seems to think that the snow will clear up soon, at least enough for us to get out the front door."

"That moment can't come soon enough, seems to me."

Beyond his annoyance at his work, there seemed to be some underlying current within him, as well, a sort of agitation. The confined quarters of the inn grated on him and he desired to be back out there in the city. Allison could certainly understand that desire. Their conversation continued in fits and starts, as it was clear that both chafed horribly at the way the past five days had transpired and were implacably irritated, neither of which tended to foster meaningful conversation.

Upon awakening on her sixth day of confinement, Allison noticed from her window that she could see gray cobblestones peaking from beneath a thin layer of snow and ice. She quickly dressed, throwing on her frock at the end and nearly forgetting her holster, which had to be belted on as she rushed down the stairs. Marcia met her halfway through the common room, but Allison strode past her with little more than a halfhearted apology and a curt "Excuse me."

The cold air of deep winter slapped her in the face straightaway. Long days beneath thick blankets or sitting beside a roaring fire had helped her forget just how bitterly cold it was outside. The snow in the street, far from melting, appeared to have been scooped away in some manner. It was still piled high on either side of the street, but a narrow lane through the middle would at least allow her to get where she needed to go.

Her mind worked. There was that alley, with the tents and makeshift shelters of the homeless, empty and deserted. But there was something which would have to come first, something which she should have done the very first day in Illdara. Mrs. Celeste had met with several wealthy families. Those families needed to be questioned. No doubt they had been already, and nothing had come of it, but the chance existed that the local police had missed something important. And now Allison had something to ask about which the local police had likely neglected.

According to the report provided by Inspector Jairyn, and which she'd found the time to read through during the past five days, the minister of finance's wife had met with three families, all of whom had mansions along Freeman's Way near the market. Getting there wasn't so hard, as the snow had been cleared away well enough and the streets were still very much empty. Though they were now no longer confined to their homes, it seemed the people of the city were still not quite willing to venture out just yet.

The market was little more than a heap of snow higher than Allison's head, but the massive houses beyond had nothing but a thin layer of snow covering roofs and grounds. Carefully placed and tended trees lined each side of Freeman's, creaking and popping whenever their bare, frozen limbs caught a gust of wind. The houses here were quite large, home to the city's wealthy elite, and largely indistinguishable from one another. High walls surrounded each home and were fronted by tightly-locked, very sturdy, iron gates. Even at such an early hour, even in such bitterly-cold weather, stone-faced guards stared back at her through the ironwork with an open suspicion.

Allison raised her copper badge at the gate to the first house, owned by the Mondale family. The guards quietly conferred with one another, then the gates swung open on well-oiled hinges. She was motioned through, then one guard got in front of her and another got behind her. The front doors swung open, silently, and all three went inside.

The foyer was under a massive dome where a sparkling chandelier dripping with crystal dangled above thick marble shot with veins of deep blue that was rather striking. And it was all very brightly lit, with hardly a shadow to be seen. Allison sat on an ornate bench along one wall and waited. And waited. And waited.

It took more than an hour, by her watch, for someone to finally appear. A servant, by the looks of him. The aging man silently motioned for her to follow. The two wandered through hallways and narrow corridors, even climbed a few stairs, all the while bearing witness to the kind of opulence and extravagance that could only have been accumulated through many long years of careful spending by someone with an amount of money that was nearly inconceivable. Practically every surface in the house sparkled with a high polish.

A door up ahead opened and Allison was ushered inside. The room was dimly lit, with only a fireplace crackling away along one wall, casting long shadows from each piece of furniture. Two high-backed chairs were resting in front of it and one of them was currently being occupied. Rows of books lined the walls from carpeted floor to ceiling.

"Sit, if you please, Detective," a low, gravely voice said. The speaker was an elderly woman, well into her twilight years, but possessing a grim sort of determination that suggested she had no intention of dying anytime soon. Allison sat in the empty chair.

"I thought it should be only a matter of time before I had the pleasure of meeting you for myself," the woman continued. "You are a bit younger than I thought you might be."

"Mrs. Mondale..."

"Lydia, if you please. And Mr. Mondale has not been of this world in many a year, so you may leave off the 'Mrs.,' as well."

"Yes, of course."

"Ask your questions."

"Very well," Allison said. "First, I'd like to know about the nature of Mrs. Victoria Celeste's visit."

Lydia sighed. "Must I go through such matters a second time?" She glanced at Allison, her gaze briefly lingering. "As I suspected. Mrs. Celeste approached my family with a proposition. She claimed to be in the possession of a great deal of money and was looking into somewhere to invest it. The girl was never overly clear about the amount, or the sort of business she wished to be involved with. Ultimately, I decided that the whole affair was nothing more than a scam. Any woman could purchase clothing as fine as hers and say that she is the wife of a prominent politician from the capital. Who are we to understand otherwise? It came as some surprise to me to learn later that she was indeed who she claimed to be."

It all seemed to fit in with what Inspector Jairyn had told her earlier, but there were still a few more questions left to be asked. "What of this money she claimed to have? Did she ever say where she happened to obtain it from?"

"No, Detective, she did not. She spoke much of the topic of money, but rarely of her own alleged fortune."

"What of her husband? Did she speak much of him?"

Lydia thought on this a moment. "A few times, in passing, but she seemed to have a strong desire to make it quite clear to me that her husband had nothing to do with this venture. Striking out on her own, away from the bureaucracy and wrangling of the capital, away from the prying eyes of an overbearing husband." With a sharp look from Allison, Lydia added, "Her words, Detective, not mine."

"Can you think of anything at all that might help my investigation?" Allison asked, pressing further. "Did she ever seem afraid or mention any enemies she may have had?"

"She mentioned nothing of the sort, nor did she ever appear to be in fear of her life. I'm afraid that is all I can help you with, Detective." Lydia made a motion with her hand towards the door and her servant reappeared to lead Allison back to the front gate.

As Allison had feared, none of her questions had elicited any information that Jairyn's men had not already obtained nearly a month ago.

Questions asked at the two other mansions, the same questions, yielded practically the same answers. Yes, Mrs. Celeste spoke of a great sum of money and a desire to invest it. No, she didn't say anything about being afraid or having any enemies. Nothing more than a waste of time better spent pursuing other matters. As she walked towards the door of the third study she'd visited that day, she stopped.

"Mr. Timsley," she said, her back still turned to the young-ish man as he sat behind an oaken desk that was far too clean and orderly to have ever been used seriously, "did Mrs. Celeste happen to mention any interest in the Duganite cult?"

"The Duganite cult?" he asked, the question seeming to take him by surprise. "No...no, I can't say that she did. There's little money to be had in such a small order, she'd not have been interested in taking her money to them. Faustus Prin's wealth is old money, accumulated by an old family. He's not known, from what I understand, to spend it often."

"Perhaps so," Allison said, "but might *they* have had an interest in her money? It must cost a great deal to purchase and operate such a large headquarters."

"Are you implying that the Duganite cult may have had something to do with this? Such an allegation is preposterous! The cult may be secretive, I agree, but that doesn't mean they're some murderous band of thugs! Unless you have some proof of this, I must ask you not to throw around such careless accusations."

"Merely a thought," Allison said, unruffled by his outburst. She turned her head slightly to see his face. "Are you, perchance, a member of the Duganites, Mr. Timsley?"

His brows went flat. "I don't see that that is any business of yours, Detective, and I fail to see how this bears any relation to your case."

"Of course, Mr. Timsley, my question stemmed merely from a passing curiosity. Good day, sir."

Chapter 10

It was highly likely that Mr. Timsley was a member of the Duganite cult, perhaps the same could even be said of the heads of the other two families, but she had no solid proof of that. Even if she did, quite a leap had to be made between that and the murder of a politician's wife. Still too many pieces that didn't fit together. But with the woefully inadequate entry for the Duganite cult in the police archives, the cult's lavish headquarters, and Mr. Timsley's reaction to her questions, she had little doubt that there was more to the Duganites than anyone was willing to admit in her presence. She could not, however, shake the feeling that she was following after an errant strand that was only leading her farther and farther away from the original murder.

Noon, according to her pocket watch. Enough of the day was still left for her to spend a number of additional hours in the cold, snow-clogged streets, asking questions and getting vague, unhelpful answers for her effort. It was hardly fair that she should be the only one working day after day on this case and coming up with nothing. Hardly fair at all, yet she was the one to whom the case had been assigned. Failure would likely mean her job and might even mean a team of detectives coming in from the capital, which would only exacerbate an already dangerous problem. And all the while, the killer would go free, perhaps even continuing in his violence.

The frigid air had already rubbed her throat raw and constantly going from outside to well-warmed interior rooms had left her with a throbbing headache centered just behind her right eye.

Allison felt around in her pocket until her hand closed on the copper ring. It felt like a solid chunk of ice against her palm, so cold that it burned. The people of this city depended on her efforts, even if they neither acknowledged nor even realized this fact. It all fell to her, for them and for all the foreigners who might suffer if the killer wasn't soon found. With no other leads, Allison determined to find again that strange alley and see what might lie below it in the city's underground labyrinth.

Before she'd gone more than a few blocks, she noticed a coach struggling to make its way through the snow-choked streets. The horses' fur was thick with clumps of snow and ice and their breath billowed out in great jets of steam. Rather than fight the rest of the way, the driver finally stopped the team and jumped down. He ran to her with the utmost haste.

"Sorry to bother you, Detective," the young man said, saluting crisply. "The coroner said to come get you right away. You weren't at the inn, so I've been searching the city for you this past hour."

"He's discovered something?"

"I reckon he has, ma'am, but he didn't tell me what it was. Just said to come find you straightaway."

They weren't far from police headquarters as it was and the horses appeared on the verge of collapse. "Get your team back inside where it's warm, I can walk there myself."

"Ah, thank you, ma'am," the young man said, clearly relieved, "thank you kindly."

Allison hurried to the morgue.

The old beggar man that had been the second victim was laid out on the one of the slabs. Conley was standing beside him and waved Allison over when she entered.

"You seemed to be in some haste to get my attention," Allison said, "have you truly found something so important?"

"Important?" Conley rubbed his chin. "Perhaps important, yes. I leave to you to decide." He pointed to the opening along the man's midsection, where his sternum had been split apart and his internal organs revealed. Thanks to the cold, rot had not yet begun to set in. "Tell what you see."

Allison bent over the old man and carefully examined his corpse. Human anatomy had been among her areas of study while at the academy, so she'd seen her share of corpses before, both inside and out, and had some idea of what everything ought to look like. All the organs appeared to be there, though some were damaged on account of the stab wounds, but the knife alone could not account for how many of them were covered in black splotches or were horribly shriveled.

"The rotting sickness?" Allison asked.

"Indeed," Conley replied. "Even without attack, this man would die in three weeks time, perhaps one month."

"He was dying...," Allison said, strange thoughts and possibilities running through her mind. "Would he have known, even at this advanced stage?"

"It is possibility," Conley said, shrugging his shoulders slightly. "Who can say? Likely his strength failed him in past weeks, bouts of coughing and sudden weakness. Rotting sickness is known, but not so common."

"It's certainly strange, Conley, but I don't see that this necessarily has any bearing on the case."

"Ah, thought that you would say so." He picked up a clipboard with several documents attached and handed it to Allison.

Allison read the documents and her eyes widened. "Mrs. Celeste had the rotting sickness, as well. Why didn't you tell me before?!"

Again Conley shrugged his shoulders. "Seemed inconsequential to case," he said. "Why would rotting sickness have bearing on murder investigation?"

"Why, indeed," Allison mumbled. One could be considered a mere accident, a cruel twist of fate that someone in their last days should be cut down in such a horrible manner. But two? No, to find two on the verge of death, a politician's wife and an old beggar, seemed far less like coincidence. Two people who couldn't be any more different, tied together by a sickness that made all men equal. It could be no coincidence, surely, but how could the killer have known?

"That I cannot say." Allison had asked that final thought aloud. "I can only tell to you facts of case, no more."

"A killer who only goes after victims already at death's door, who leaves behind bizarre clues, and who kills with a ceremonial dagger of some kind." And who leaves behind cryptic warnings to the foreign detective in charge of the case. "What could all these things possibly add up to?"

Conley took the clipboard and set it aside. With care, he redid the stitches along the old beggar's chest, closing him up again, and then pulled a plain, white cloth up over his face. "No more he has to tell us, I think. It is time now for him to sleep."

Conley's two assistants entered and helped to carry the body towards the far end of the room, where the heat from a great fire glowed orange against the plain, white walls. Albert Brimley, a man with little money and no home to call his own, would join Victoria Celeste, the wife of the capital's minister of finance, in those roaring flames.

Allison stood in the street again, feet and hands slowly turning numb, face freezing, still no closer to an answer than she had been upon waking that morning. Two in the afternoon, by her watch. Still time, time enough for yet more thankless work to be done. Another clue, another piece, but the puzzle remained far from being complete. The day's work had left her feeling numb inside and out, so she walked aimlessly.

Her feet took her down to the docks, where she entered the seediest dive she could find. Rough and mean, nearly every table in the ramshackle bar was filled with burly sailors deep into their drinks. No more than one or two even glanced in her direction as she walked past their tables. A quiet, secluded corner of the bar was empty. The noise, the din of voices all talking at once, grew and grew as evening turned to night.

Tales were told--the bawdier the better--and songs were sung, many of them very old songs that Allison had heard a time or two back at the capital. A wide variety of them, some sad and some happy, but all sang with the same sort of exuberance, the same flippant attitude, that only the amount of alcohol commonly drank to forget about the world could afford. Whatever may have been going on the city, whatever might come tomorrow, these men lived in the moment, and that moment was drenched in an alcoholic haze that would soon put them under well into the next day. Not one of the sailors spoke of the city or the murders. In a way, that was telling in itself.

With the sun gone and the city dark, Allison wandered north. The great bell tower rang out the time, ten o'clock. She found a low wall just off the road near the lighthouse and waited. As she'd hoped, the Duganites came as they had before. They slowly filed past her, as silent as ghosts. At the lighthouse, they turned to the right and continued down through a pair of sturdy doors. When the last of them went through, the doors were shut.

Allison hurried over and tried the doors. They were both shut tight and rebuffed all her efforts to open them. She could see nothing at all on her side that appeared to be a lock. She poked around at the base of the lighthouse for a while longer, but found no other entrance to the Duganite's secret lair or any sort of clue that would help her understand what it was they did down there each night.

Allison returned to the inn, but she wasn't tired. For several hours, she lay on her bed and stared at the ceiling. It was not thoughts of the case that kept her awake, but the long hours and days she'd spent resting during the snowstorm that had nearly buried the city. She could probably search the rest of the night and still not truly be tired. She could search the rest of the night and still find nothing that would help her solve this case.

Her thoughts turned to her father and she remember being young, watching him put on his coat, shine his boots, and carefully place the copper badge on his left breast each morning. The pride in his eyes as he stood before the mirror, ensuring that nothing was out of order, had been so evident to her, even back then. She remembered the smile he gave her as he turned to shut the front door, always a smile for his beloved daughter. And she remembered the day he died, digging too deeply into a case that he'd been warned about. An unfortunate attack by a desperate crook just looking for some quick money, the investigator said. The file was closed, her father was buried. Unconsciously, Allison touched the badge still resting in her pocket. It was always polished. Always.

Someone knocked at her door, so low and so quiet that she almost didn't hear it from within the depths of all those old, faded memories.

"Is someone there?" she asked, sitting up.

"I must speak with you, Detective."

Allison quickly lit the lantern sitting beside her bed and then cracked the door open just slightly. Though the figure on the other side wore a long cloak with the hood drawn, she could see enough of the face to know who it was.

"Blake Timsley."

The Illdaran noble glanced nervously towards each end of the hall. Allison opened the door wider and he practically trampled her to get inside. Once the door was shut, he pulled back his hood.

"I'm taking a great risk in coming to see you here, Detective," he said, "I hope you can appreciate that."

"That depends on what you came here for, Mr. Timsley," Allison said, gesturing towards one of the two chairs in the room. Mr. Timsley graciously took her up on the offer, shaking a bit of the snow from his cloak as he did so.

"The Duganite cult," he said, "you wish to know about them?"

Allison wordlessly nodded her head.

Mr. Timsley paused a moment to glance at the door, as if to reassure himself that it was truly closed. "I know something of them," he said at last, "of their rituals and their ways." He looked up at her. "It was fear that held my tongue before, but I've found that I cannot bear to keep the secret any longer."

"Tell me what you know."

He nodded his head at this. "The Duganite cult worships the sea, as I'm sure Faustus Prin told you, but what they did not tell you is that there is one who dwells in the sea and it is to him that their prayers and sacrifices are made."

"It's not so strange for them to worship a lord of the sea," Allison said, "even the Temple has such a god in its pantheon."

Mr. Timsley vigorously shook his head. A great fear had taken hold of him that Allison had not seen before. This man was not merely nervous or agitated, he was terrified. "Not like this," he said, his voice shaking, "not like this." He paused to draw breath. "I saw him once, only once, during a ceremony, a...sacrificial ceremony. They spoke of raising him, of bringing him...*it*...back into the world." His eyes grew wider as he relived whatever it was he'd experienced. "You cannot imagine it, Detective! You cannot! Paragar is an abomination, a creature beyond all our abilities to comprehend! It's powers are...are..." His entire body shook and his jaw slowly worked, but no sounds or words came forth.

Allison leaned over and put her hands on his shoulders, looking him directly in the eye. He jerked as his eyes moved slowly to meet hers and then remained locked there.

"You mean to tell me that the god they worship is no spiritual being, but a thing with physical form? Is that what you're telling me?"

His head bobbled back and forth.

"These sacrifices they made...what were they?"

"I...I don't know. I don't know! Never saw...I never saw them, I swear!"

Allison eased down into the other chair.

"Is there anything more you can tell me?" she asked. "Even something small or something that might seem insignificant to you?"

"No," he said. "No, I've said too much already. If they knew...they...I've said too much."

He stood, then, pulling his hood back down over his face. "Th-thank you for listening to me ramble on. Please excuse me."

Without waiting for her reply, he went to the door, wrenched it open, and was gone back down the hallway before Allison could even think to stop him. She walked to the door and watched as he disappeared down the steps. A light burned in the room across from her.

Chapter 11

Blake Timsley never made it back home. When morning came, his family reported him missing. He'd simply left the inn and then...disappeared. Chief Inspector Jairyn took the matter seriously, as seriously as he took everything, but refused to speculate about what might have happened to the wealthy nobleman. There was no body this time, no clues to follow. His family didn't even known that he'd gone out for the night.

The talk in the common room at the inn was not quite so muted as it had been after the second murder, but people were talking. Speculation ran rampant as to what might have happened to poor Blake Timsley. It was a mystery, another clue in a puzzle that grew larger with each passing day.

Two murders, that she knew of; two disappearances, that she knew of. A murderer running loose through the city and a strange cult bent on resurrecting some abyssal horror, if the words of a man who'd slowly come unhinged in the telling of that wild tale could be believed. Such people seemed to be the only ones to give her straight answers. Despite all these pieces, none of it added up to very much. Not enough to make any sort of arrest, which was all Allison truly hoped for at that point.

Allison spent several hours in a meeting with Inspector Jairyn, telling him about her visit from Blake Timsley just before his disappearance, though she kept a few things back. The inspector ought to know that he'd come to her, but he didn't necessarily need to know everything.

"Might the Duganite cult have had some reason to want him gone?" Allison asked.

"The Duganites do not cause trouble in this city, Detective," Inspector Jairyn replied, fingers intertwined in front of his face.

"Perhaps all that's changed recently? You yourself admit that little is known of the cult, a fact borne out by their file in the archives. If so little is known, how can you be so sure they had nothing to do with Mr. Timsley's disappearance? Or even the two murders? Perhaps Mr. Timsley learned something and they threatened him. After he came to me, they decided to shut him up for good!"

"Enough!" Inspector Jairyn exclaimed. "You're here to find evidence to solve a murder, not throw about baseless accusations. If you find the evidence to link the two, then we'll have more to say. If that's all, you may leave now, I've much work to do today."

Allison turned to leave, but stopped at the door, half-opened. "Do you happen to know a girl by the name of Julia Ahbin?"

"Never heard of her," he said, face unreadable.

"Good day, Chief Inspector."

Back in the streets, Allison already knew what it was she wanted to do.

A general store was open not far from police headquarters, run by a man determined to squeeze some small amount of profit out of a dire situation. He looked surprised, nevertheless, to see her enter. There was a brief conflict, no doubt brought upon by the knowledge that she was not of Illdara, but that ultimately lost out in light of his desperation to make a sale, any sale, to whoever happened through the door.

The purchase of a lantern and some extra oil was made and Allison was soon on her way back to the alley she'd investigated before the snow storm. With all the snow piled everywhere, it was hard to figure out exactly where the alley was located, so she spent nearly two hours pushing through tall drifts and the city's spidery network of alleys before finally recognizing a few buildings. The fire that had burned in the alley some six days ago had gone out and the makeshift shelters were buried beneath nearly six feet of snow.

With some effort, Allison managed to dig away enough of the powdery drifts to get down to the cobblestones. The metal disc, sealing the tunnel that led down, was where she remembered it being, though it had become almost completely frozen in place. Some of the ice had to be chipped away with her knife. Another half hour passed away before the dark chasm was finally exposed to meager daylight.

Allison lit the lantern and slid her arm through the metal ring used to carry it. Then she climbed down into the narrow chasm, pulling the metal disc back into place. Anyone happening upon that particular alley would notice straightaway that someone had gone down into the underground, but leaving the chasm open felt wrong somehow.

The dull ringing of her boots as they bumped against each rung echoed along the length of the chasm. The faint dripping of water somewhere in the distance, her own labored breathing. Thirty rungs, more than forty-five feet, before her boots finally touched solid ground again-- carved stones held together by a rough mortar, from the look of it. The sound of flowing water reached her ears, then, from down where it was not quite so cold as up above. It was almost warm down there, humid and damp. Corridors ran in either direction, continuing beyond the light of her lantern.

Here was where her training as a detective would come in handy, here where there were no obvious signs of which direction she ought to go in, no obvious clues pointing towards the answer. It all came down to instinct, that deeply-ingrained feeling that tugged gently at the back of the mind and whispered hints and advice with a barely-audible voice. Allison looked one way, then another. Her feet carried her forward.

Most of the tunnels looked the same. Carved stones on either side, curving upward towards the ceiling. A narrow channel in the middle, a step down from the elevated paths. Some of them carried water, or other foul-smelling liquids, but many were dry. No signs, no clues, no indications, no matter how carefully she looked.

Minutes and hours slowly drained away as Allison trudged through narrow, faceless, unmarked tunnels whose ceilings were so low that she was forced to stoop nearly in half. The thick, choking stench of the place made the going no easier, nor did the oppressive darkness that lurked just outside the ring of feeble light cast by her lantern.

She found no chambers down there, no massive rooms with towering ceilings, as she'd heard the underground in the capital was like, only those same tunnels, branching off in every direction like the silken web of a spider. Allison continued, directionless and lost.

However, her search did lead her to a room that stood out from everything else: a room of levers, valves, and complicated machinery that gulped and wheezed and rattled out a hideous tune. Flammable gas hissed through a maze of pipes that came through the walls, floor, and ceiling. It was a central switching room for the lights that kept the streets of Illdara from total darkness, perhaps even kept the homeless warm during the long, winter months. But nothing was marked and the room was unoccupied, though she did find signs that the room was used and quite regularly. It was certainly interesting, a break from the monotony of the underground, but it held no clues for her.

As afternoon passed into evening, Allison paused to rest for a moment. The area she found herself in was much like all the other parts of the underground she'd seen, except that there was a narrow set of stone steps leading even deeper into the ground, to some, as yet unseen, network of tunnels and passages. For a time, she sat and stared at those steps, wondering just how much longer the fuel in her lantern would last.

Faint scratches that marred the stones managed to catch her eye. She drew closer and brushed away some clinging lichen that partially obscured them. With the scratches fully uncovered, it became quite obvious that it was no natural phenomenon, nor even the act of some animal or another. The scratches formed a shaky arrow, pointing down the steps. The markings weren't new.

Any misgivings she'd had before about venturing deeper into the underground vanished almost in an instant. Allison felt at her belt for the flintlock pistol, to reassure herself that it was still there, and then carefully descended the narrow steps. The edges were rounded, showing a great deal more wear than she'd yet seen in the underground. People came through here, a lot of people and fairly often.

Even being very generous, this went far beyond the bounds of what might be considered a part of her murder investigation. She was groping in the dark, almost literally, for clues and hints, even where she felt that surely there must be none at all. It was a desperate move to even consider this venture, more desperate still to actually go forward with it. How much more foolish, then, was it to go ever deeper into these trackless bowels as the fuel for her lantern slowly burned away?

But Allison pressed on, moving through tunnels that grew smaller and smaller, tunnels that pressed against her shoulders and forced her to crawl on her hands and knees. Above all else, she determined to find something, anything, that would somehow make all her effort worthwhile.

As day turned to night, according to her pocket watch, she began to see light up ahead, piercing through the inky darkness like the rising sun. She extinguished her own lantern and then crawled closer to that light, closer to what it might reveal.

The tunnel ended suddenly, opening into a vast chamber lit by roaring fires. A great pool of water covered much of the far end, bubbling faintly as if there might be something alive in those murky, unseen depths. And there were people, as well, nearly thirty in all, wearing dark robes and silvery masks that gleamed in the firelight.

A ceremony of some kind appeared to be ongoing. Amidst the roaring bonfires, candles also burned: great, smokey candles that gave off a pungent odor Allison could smell all the way at the back of the chamber. Someone was speaking, possibly Faustus Prin.

The tunnel mouth was suspended some fifteen feet above the floor, with little below but a quick drop to hard stones, but Allison spotted a ledge that ran the length of the chamber to her left, just above her head. If she pulled herself along the ledge, she'd eventually reach a set of stone steps not too far away. There was always the chance that she'd fall and have to deal with two broken legs or that she'd be spotted almost immediately, but she'd already come this far. It wouldn't do to just back out.

With care, she reached out to the ledge, grasping it in her hands, and then pulled the rest of her body out of the tunnel. Her legs swung precariously, threatening to rip her hands loose, but she quickly pulled them back in as her fingernails scratched against the cold stone. A ragged breath taken, she slowly moved one hand and then another. Her feet dangled uselessly, finding no hold on the slick, flat wall.

Then finally, the steps were beneath her feet. She dropped down and then quickly turned, looking for any signs that she'd been spotted. The speech continued unabated, she'd not been seen.

Broken stumps of ancient pillars and other rubble littered the floor of the chamber, suggesting that a structure had once existed down there. No indication remained as to what it may have looked like or been used for. Allison made her way closer to the band of cultists until she could finally hear the speaker's words.

"...very soon now," she heard the man say. The voice sounded like it might have belonged to Faustus Prin, but the words were muffled by his intricately-carved mask. "All our trials and tribulations, all our dedication and prayers, shall at last be answered." He paused, as if to gather himself. "Words came to me this past night, the words of Paragar, our Lord and Master, telling me this great news. We are so close now, my brothers, close to raising the tide which will sweep across the land and destroy the abominations that this world has so carelessly brought forth. This I swear in my heart, this I believe with all my will. May the sea shelter and protect us, may its bounty ever feed us." He bowed his head low, as did all the others.

Allison inched back away from the group, fearing they might be close to disbanding for the night. Their moment of silence ended and Faustus' face rose. He turned slightly to his left and nodded almost imperceptibly. From a side passage shrouded in darkness, two cultists appeared, hidden beneath long robes and behind silvery masks, dragging behind them a young girl.

She appeared drugged, her eyes listless and dull in the faint light. She was thin, practically wasting away; her clothes were tattered and dirty, hardly more than rags; and her face was smudged with grime. She didn't resist.

The speaker raised a hand, fingers pointing to a flat slab of stone jutting from out of the floor and adorned with metal rings, to which the girl's arms and legs were tied. She did not look at any of them and instead merely stared straight ahead, eyes unseeing.

From beneath the robe of the speaker, he produced a long, slender blade, curved and sharp with uneven edges. An ornamental dagger. He raised it above the girl, holding it aloft as it caught the faint light of several dozen flickering candles. An ornamental dagger. Allison gasped and her voice echoed through the chamber.

"Who dares to disturb our sacred ceremony?!" the speaker roared, his voice shaking the walls of the chamber like a sudden peal of thunder.

Allison leapt to her feet and scrambled up the aging steps. The cultists came directly behind her, their robes flapping as they ran. The steps felt more and more like the sheer face of a mountain as she climbed higher. Her pursuers were moving so rapidly that they reached the bottom of the steps before she'd even reached the middle. A surge of fear pushed her forward and she scrambled up the last few steps, coming to a long hallway. Without thought, Allison ran.

The echoes of boots and angry shouts pounded at her from all sides, seeming as though they originated from only a few feet behind. An iron door appeared, no handle. Allison threw her weight against it and the door flung open, slamming into the wall. A small room, lit with a single candle. Few adornments, nothing of interest. Stairs led upward. She rushed up the stairs and found them blocked by another door. But this door had a handle. With a quick twist, the doors flew open.

Crashing waves and the wind coming off the sea, welcome sounds. Allison stood at the base of the lighthouse. With her boot, she kicked the doors shut again, even as the cultists, bearing torches, entered the tiny room below. Allison ran.

The streets were empty, dark, more unfriendly than ever. Allison looked over her shoulder a hundred times as she ran back along those streets, making for the safety of the King's Crown. But she never saw any signs of pursuit, no shouts echoing off the buildings around her or glow of torches in the distance. Even so, her heart raced, hammering against her ribs so hard that it hurt. She'd been witness to the sacrifice that Mr. Timsley had spoken about, of that fact she had no doubt.

Somehow it all tied together. The cult, the murders, the disappearances. It all tied together in one neat, little package. At least, that was what she desperately wished for. Taking on such a cult would be no easy task, however, not if they had the support that Allison believed they had. This matter went deep, too deep for one foreigner to possibly handle alone. Deep enough to be killed over.

More than halfway back to the inn, Allison stopped, leaning against the wall of a building for support as her sides heaved. Too much exertion in too little time, her body just couldn't handle it all, certainly not with it being so dreadfully cold. Ahead of her, a streetlight burned, exuding a ring of welcome light. A figure appeared, standing beside the narrow pole. No more than twenty feet away, but the glare of the light in such darkness was too blinding for Allison to make out any details.

"A wonderful show," the figure said. The voice was low, barely audible as it drifted through the night air. "The most entertainment you're likely to get in this dreadful town. But don't let their costumes and gaudy pomp blind you to the truth. They meant for you to see all that, Detective, and saw it you did."

"Who are you?!" Allison demanded, too tired and too cold to wonder at anything else.

"A friend?" A dry chuckle. "No, just a stranger with friendly advice. You're getting close, Detective, very close. It won't be much longer."

Allison could feel the cold air slicing at her throat, rubbing it raw with each ragged breath. She wouldn't be able to give chase if the figure fled. Maybe if she could keep him talking long enough, she'd be able to think of something. Even so, she felt a flood of questions that threatened to overwhelm her. "What was that ceremony all about? What were they going to do with that girl? Why would they have wanted me to see it?"

"Now, now, Detective, that would be telling. You'll have to figure the answers out for yourself." The figure vanished into the darkness.

Chapter 12

After a long soak in hot water that was almost too hot to bear, Allison returned to her room at the King's Crown Inn. For a long time, she stared at the ceiling. The mystery was deepening, becoming more complex as new threads entered and the old threads became more tangled. Somehow all of it seemed to fit together, somehow none of it seemed to fit together. A cult that offered human sacrifices. A man on the loose who'd already murdered twice and who was leading her along towards...something. They fit, somehow they fit, but she just couldn't see it.

Her first thought was to go to Chief Inspector Jairyn at first light and tell him everything, round up as many officers as they could, and then break down the doors of Faustus Prin's home to force some straight answers out of him. But the thought didn't last. Inspector Jairyn wasn't her friend, or a close ally offering his support and willing to back her up. He might even have some connections to the cult. Who, then, did that leave?

It left her, Allison Newberry, alone against a city that was becoming increasingly hostile. Even if the cult couldn't tell for sure that she'd been the one to discover their secret ceremony, they likely had guessed it. If they believed some sort of aquatic "god" was preparing to rise from the sea and bring to them some manner of glory, the threat of an army of police from the capital might not be enough to deter them from ridding themselves of an overly-curious outsider, not when they'd have several months to be rid of her corpse and to come up with a suitable excuse for her death. They might not attack the inn directly, but she had to go back outside eventually and the streets were looking rather empty of late.

And just what was it that she was getting close to? The hooded figure, the same man who had killed Mrs. Celeste and the homeless man, unless Allison's instincts failed her, talked as if she'd come very close to uncovering something important. But what? And why should they have wanted her to witness their ceremony?

Allison rubbed at her eyes with the palms of her hands. It didn't make any sense! Too many pieces, too few answers. Finally, she got up in the darkened room and sat down with her back against the door. They'd at least have great difficulty in climbing all the way up to her window.

She finally knew how her father had felt in those last few days. He hadn't spoken to her about the case, but she'd see the tiredness in his eyes and the weight that pressed against his shoulders. Some nights he didn't even come home. On that last morning, he'd been afraid. She saw it so clearly in him that she'd wanted to cry. But he still flashed her that smile on the way out the door. Her father was terrified, but he still pinned on his badge, belted his gun around his waist, and walked out the front door to keep the investigation alive.

Cradling the flintlock pistol across her lap, Allison stayed awake well into the night.

The streets were mostly free of snow the next morning, but still empty. It felt as though the entire city were empty, as if the inhabitants had all vanished during the snow storm. Even the boisterous common room at the inn, filled with the smell of fried eggs and sizzling bacon, did little to shake the feeling. A momentary mirage, the distant shimmer of water fooling the thirsty traveler into a delusion that ended all too soon. Sitting in the corner, picking at a plate of food, Allison felt very much alone.

"You work much too hard, love," Martin said, pulling back an empty chair.

"I don't know how much more of this city I can take," Allison replied, not looking up from her plate.

"Getting to you already? It happens, I've seen it for myself."

"I don't know what to do, Martin."

He paused for a moment, settling back into his chair. "Can't really help you there, love. But you ought to know better than anyone else what it is a detective needs to do in this situation. And if your training doesn't tell you, well...," he shrugged, "then you must let your instincts light your way."

Allison raised her eyes. Martin smiled faintly, just enough so that she could see it. In this horrible city, it was enough to know that someone was out there who had her back, who didn't mind that she was from out of town, and who understood a bit of what it felt like to be in her situation. More than two hundred leagues from home, Martin truly was the only friend she had.

Allison took a long drink from her stein and then set it aside.

"Thanks, Martin."

"Sure enough, love," Martin said as she walked away. "Just you make sure you come back at the end of the day, this city would be far too loncly without you."

Just on the other side of the front door to the inn, Allison checked her pistol, her father's pistol that hadn't been fired in fifteen years of service. It still rested at her side, always loaded and always ready, should the need arise. Her copper badge was pushed down into a pocket of her frock, freshly polished. She touched it lightly, reminding herself that it really was still there. Whatever else, she was a detective in the King's service, trained to solve crimes and bring the perpetrators back to face the justice they deserved. In Illdara, there was still a crime waiting to be solved.

With little to go on, Allison went to the docks, to the packed ale houses and inns, and asked questions of anyone willing, and even a few unwilling, to give her their attention. She asked about the murders, the Duganites, and anything else that seemed remotely connected to either. Prowling from one drunken sailor to the next, she was given short shrift by them all. Their desire to talk was limited, their desire to answer questions on the topics about which Allison wanted information even more so.

When the mood in one place began to sour, and Allison began to draw too much attention to herself, she'd leave and go to the next. There was no shortage of wide, open rooms filled with chairs and tables and sailors with jingling pouches, where alcohol of one kind or another was served in great abundance.

Morning gave way to afternoon. Afternoon gave way to evening. Word of her questioning spread. Soon, no one would talk to her, even in the taverns she'd not yet gone into. They ignored her, even when she raised her voice. This continued up to the third such tavern, outside of which Allison was met by two large men. Their shoulders were broad, their chins square, and their arms exposed to the freezing air, each displaying an impressive set of muscles. One of the two had a nose that looked to have been broken multiple times.

"You will come with us," said the one with the busted nose, in a manner that suggested she wasn't being given a choice.

"And where am I to come with you to?"

"You want to talk, eh? Our boss will talk."

It was painfully clear that she'd begun to make a nuisance of herself and that going with these two gentlemen might not be in her best interests, but there was also the possibility that their "boss" might actually have a true desire to speak with her. Resting her hand on the butt of her pistol, she said, "Lead on."

The two men led her along the docks for a way, then turned onto one of the long, thin fingers that extended out into the bay. Tied up at the end was an imposing ship, made of dark wood and adorned with three tall masts bristling with furled sails. It swayed gently in the half-frozen waters as the rigging creaked and moaned. No crewmen were about, at least that she could see.

They led her up the gang plank and onto the deck, then down several steps through a wooden door at the front of the quarterdeck. Several narrow corridors took them to the back of the ship, to the captain's quarters. One of the men pushed the door open and the other pushed Allison inside. They shut the door behind her.

The captain's quarters were spacious, luxurious even. Large, nautical maps hung from the walls beside naval weapons, bones from some great aquatic beast, and several flags of various patterns and colors. The bed in the corner was canopied and thick with padding, no less expensive than the ornately-carved desk resting in front of three broad windows, where the curtains were pushed back to bathe the room in

Illdara's meager light. Amidst it all was the captain, lounging in a high-backed chair with a tightly-wound cigar clenched between his teeth.

"Sit," the captain said, gesturing to an empty chair resting in front of his desk.

Allison sat.

"My men tell me you've been stirring things up lately, a bit too much, perhaps," the captain said.

"I should like to know who I'm speaking with before this conversation goes any further," Allison said crisply.

The captain folded his hands in front of his face, the corners of his lips curling up slightly. "Garrus Locklain, harbormaster for Illdara's port during these long, winter months."

"And you know already who I am?"

Garrus nodded. "Too well," he said, "but pleasantries are not why I asked you here."

"Then why *did* you ask me here?"

He took a long draw from his cigar and then ground it into a golden ashtray. "You've been asking questions, a lot of questions, and it's got people stirred up. They're starting to think something's going on and that's making them nervous. It's bad enough that the locals are starting to look askance at every sailor in the city, thinking each and every one of them's hiding a knife in his boot and is eager to use it."

"I'm doing the job that His Majesty employs me to do," Allison said, the implications of the conversation grating on her, "nothing more."

"And how could I possibly begrudge you that, Detective? I invited you to my ship so that I may answer your questions here and now, rather than allow you to continue your vain search and bother my men."

"If you know something of the murder or of the Duganite cult, then speak. I'm sure your time is no less precious than mine."

Garrus smiled, but there was no humor in it, more like the toothy grin of a shark as it bears down on its prey. Any help he might give her would not come as a favor, as the man very much expected to get something out of all this. Even so, Allison currently had no leads worth wasting thought on, so she remained quiet and listened.

"The Duganite cult," Captain Locklain said, "but not so much the murder. If there's a connection, and I believe you think one exists, it'll be up to you to find it and prove it. Now, I've had dealings with the cult and with Faustus Prin, enough to know that I want no further dealings with them, if I can help it."

He reached across his desk to a small box, flipping up the lid and pulling out another cigar. With skillful precision, he clipped off the end and lit the cigar with a long match in several smooth motions. He offered one to Allison, who quickly waved it away.

"The Duganites worship the sea, specifically they worship something they call 'Paragar,' an aquatic god of one kind or another. Nasty, is the word for it. They told me it's a great, bulbous thing sprouting countless tentacles, blind and cruel. They offer sacrifices to it in secret ceremonies, burn incense, slaughter animals, and so on. But somebody once told me that it goes further than that, that the Duganites sometimes take a human with them and cast it into a pool of water where they believe Paragar dwells. Tentacles drift up to surface and drag the poor soul down into the deep...where Paragar feeds. I've never seen such a ceremony myself and have no desire to, if it exists."

"There...may be some truth in what you say, Captain Locklain," Allison said, feeling acutely the trembling in her hands.

"Hmm...," the captain said. If he noticed her trembling, he didn't acknowledge it. "There is one more thing I can tell you, but you'll have to decide the truth of it for yourself. The Duganite cult is searching for someone, a living sacrifice. They seem to believe that sacrificing a certain individual to Paragar will raise him from his watery tomb at last, to flood the world and bring about a new age. A different kind of sacrifice, for a different kind of purpose." Garrus shrugged his shoulders. "It sounds like a great deal of nonsense to me, but perhaps they do truly believe such rubbish. Whether any of this helps you, I can't say, but now you know as much as anyone outside of the cult members themselves."

"They hold a great deal of power in Illdara, don't they?" Allison asked, barely able to say the words. "Influence with the right people, vast riches. They wouldn't be above ridding themselves of someone to preserve their secrets?"

Garrus took a long draw form his cigar, his eyes never leaving her. "If they were not watching you before, Allison Newberry, then surely they will be watching you after today."

"Thank you, Captain Locklain," Allison mumbled. She stood from her chair and left the captain's quarters, not bothering to say any more or to wait for him to bid her leave. It all fit with what she'd seen with her own eyes, what she'd heard Faustus Prin say in the bowels of Illdara. Kidnappings for their horrible rituals, human sacrifices.

They'd meant for her to see it, but why? And this living sacrifice...Faustus seemed to be hinting that they were coming very close to finding this individual. In a number of ways, it all meant that time was of the essence. She could not afford to let this mystery dangle unsolved for much longer.

Even so, it was difficult to truly believe it all. The words of a stranger in the night, of a ship captain looking to gain something, of the mad leader of a band of cultists. How could she trust the words of any of these three? She was left with nothing but to take what she knew to Chief Inspector Jairyn and ask him directly.

The inspector happened to still be in his office even though it was well into the evening. He was in the process of poring over a large number of reports and did not immediately notice that she'd entered.

"Inspector, we need to talk," Allison said.

Inspector Jairyn slammed a stack of reports down on his desk. "What now?" he demanded.

"I need to know about the Duganite cult."

"There's nothing to say, Detective. They keep to themselves and don't make a fuss. If you want to join their little band, then ask them directly."

"Inspector, I *know* you're hiding something from me. The Duganite cult is not some harmless group, as you say. Far from it, in fact. I have reason to believe that they've been involved in several disappearances in Illdara and may even have a close connection to the murders of Victoria Celeste and Albert Brimley."

"You still won't drop that angle?" the inspector asked. "I told you once already to bring me evidence and keep your *speculation* to yourself!"

"I've seen with my own eyes what they do!" Allison snapped. "Human sacrifice to Paragar, their 'god.'"

Inspector Jairyn leaned back in his chair. "Fine," he said. "Let's assume for the moment that there's some validity to your claims. Who, exactly, is missing? I have no unsolved disappearances currently in the cold case files."

"You've found Blake Timsley?"

"Yes, Detective, we have," Inspector Jairyn said. "His body was found washed up in the harbor this morning. One of his wrists was slashed and a number of his bones were shattered. Most likely he threw himself from the cliffs and died immediately upon hitting the rocks below."

Allison frowned. "Why wasn't I told?"

"Because it was never your investigation, Detective. *Murder* is what you're supposed to be solving, though I've seen little evidence to suggest you've been doing that."

Allison put her hands on the chief inspector's desk and leaned forward. "It's highly likely that Blake Timsley *was* murdered."

"By the Duganites, you mean to say?" Inspector Jairyn came very close to sneering. "When I went to the family with news of his death, they finally told me the truth. Mr. Blake Timsley has not been of sound mind for some time. He's been prone to fits and spells, bouts of madness of some kind. They'd forgotten to lock his door the night he came to see you, the night he took his own life. His own madness was his end, Detective."

"I'd like to see the body."

"Then go pester Conley."

Allison very nearly stormed out of the room to go find the coroner, but stopped short. "What about Julia Ahbin? Have you discovered her, as well?"

One of the inspector's brows rose. "That name again? There's nothing mysterious about her case."

"Last time I asked, you said you knew nothing of her."

"Indeed," the chief inspector said blandly, "but I decided to look through our old records. Out of personal curiosity. There's really nothing to say, Detective. The girl took twenty silver pieces from her employer and fled on one of the ships that left during the spring thaw. I even have sworn testimony from the captain of that vessel saying that he did indeed find such a girl stowed away on board, but continued on with her to their next port, as she paid him with two silver pieces for her passage."

"Her former boyfriend seems to think differently."

Inspector Jairyn didn't blink. "Geoffrey Merrin would be on Ellsberth Island right now if the asylum were still open. He's a very disturbed young man and caused quite a scene after learning this his girlfriend had fled the city."

"And that's all you have to say on the matter?" Allison asked.

"That's all there *is* to say, Detective. You have no evidence of anything, so I will not entertain these wild stories of yours."

Allison slammed the copper ring down on his desk. "If she ran away, then how did her ring end up the basement of a closed-up flower shop beneath a pile of old rags?"

Inspector Jairyn didn't even look at it. "I suspect she tossed it away and someone happened upon it."

The inspector's face was blank and unreadable. He might have been a seething pot of rage or he might have been perfectly calm, it was impossible to tell from either his voice or the set of his face. Not even his eyes gave a thing away.

"I know what I've seen, Inspector. If you're shielding the Duganites, this won't end well for you. I'll see to it that they're punished for whatever crimes they've committed *and* I'll see to that our murderer receives his justice, as well."

"I had hoped," Inspector Jairyn said, "that the capital would send one of their best, a seasoned detective with years of experience and a proven record of solved cases. Unfortunately, they did not."

Allison slammed the door to his office on her way out.

Chapter 13

Night in Illdara, the streets empty and cold. Flickering lights evenly-spaced along the major roads were just enough to see by. Allison stalked those lonely streets, seething with anger. Angry at herself for not having the proof she needed, angry at Inspector Jairyn for not giving her even an ounce of trust, angry at the city for its unrelenting hostility.

Allison returned to the King's Crown and went to her room. For a long time, she lay on her bed and stared at the ceiling. Her mind cleared, draining of emotion and thoughts of the case. The bell tolled eight o'clock and Allison knew what it was that she needed to do.

Under cover of darkness, Allison slipped out of the King's Crown without being seen. She slid through the darkened streets, avoiding those pools of light that would give her away. So many cold, faceless buildings, so many empty streets, so many darkened windows. The city was totally silent. The wind had died down and the tossing of the waves against the rocky shore was quieted at last by the choking ice that had descended from the north. No one walked those streets except for Detective Allison Newberry.

And then she arrived at the home of Faustus Prin. A few scattered lights burned in the windows, but not at all as bright as she'd seen it before. In this cold and at this hour, she hoped that everyone was already asleep and Faustus himself gone off to do the things that he and his cult did. Allison walked the perimeter, looking for easy entrance, but found none. Oh, there was entrance, sure enough, but not easy.

Around back of the building, the wall met the cliffs and extended a few feet beyond, out over the dark abyss. No wall covered the back of the property, for there was no need with the sheer cliff abutting it. Allison carefully lowered herself over the edge, tentatively probing the craggy face with her boots. The cold had at least frozen the moisture that would usually cling to the cliff face, but now she had to deal with grasping and grabbing at solid ice. She inched lower, allowing more and more of her body to slide out over the sea far below. At least with it being night, she'd not have to see just how far it was to the bottom.

Her fingers burned as they touched the frozen rock and they trembled against that horrible cold. Her boots had found a narrow purchase, just enough to support her weight and little more. Without the moon, she could scarcely see anything more than a foot away from her face. She moved one hand, carefully, searching for another handhold. If only she'd thought to bring gloves.

After only a few seconds, her muscles began to protest. A cold sweat formed on her brow and then froze before it could fall. Yet she held to the cliff. Each foothold was like a lifeline thrown from above and each clung to as if it were the only thing keeping her alive. Far too much truth resided in that analogy. Allison moved so slowly, so very slowly, that each second was an hour and each beat of her heart was the distant, intermittent rumble of thunder.

She passed the end of the wall at last, now she need only climb up and over the edge of the cliff. Her fingers had grown numb, a layer of ice thickened over them. Her muscles screamed at her to let go, to let them rest. Her head felt like it was on fire. She reached up, not knowing whether her hands were gripping anything at all. Her left boot slipped away from the rocks and her heart stopped. This was the end, wasn't it? A slip right at the very end and that was it.

In an act of desperation, she threw her right hand above her head and grabbed for something, anything. Her right boot came away from the wall, she was floating. For a brief instance, she was no longer a part of the world, but rather drifting through a darkness as black as midnight. Her fingers closed around a thick clump of dry grass, the sturdy roots held firm.

A shudder ran through her entire body and she breathed again. With her legs dangling uselessly, she quickly pulled herself up over the lip of the cliff and then rolled over on her back. For a long time, she just lay there, breathing in and breathing out. She was a right fool, no question.

A quick search of the exterior revealed that the doors and windows were all locked rather tightly. If she had all night to work, she might be able to get through a door before sunrise. Though the windows looked ornate, they'd been just as much built with security in mind, with thick glass and hard wood to keep out unwanted visitors. So, Allison searched lower to the ground, looking for an entrance into the basement that might not receive as much notice.

The bell tolled ten o'clock and Allison found a narrow window resting on the ground, partially obscured by grass. It was locked, of course, but it was not quite so sturdy as the other windows. Allison took off her coat and pressed it against the window, then she broke it out with a rock.

With the jagged glass scraped away, Allison stuck her head through the window and looked around. A few tall candles gave off flickering light, illuminating a long, narrow room with columns on either side and a blood-red rug that ran the length. An altar of some kind sat at the far end, showing signs of having been scorched by fire. Allison pulled herself through the window and dropped to the floor behind one of the columns.

The candles had clearly been burning for some time, as evidenced by the pools of hardened wax that had formed around the base of each. The room itself was clean and well-kept, likely seeing heavy use by the Duganites for some ritual or another. The door leading up to the main house was locked fast with a complicated mechanism and the door itself was made of very thick wood. No use dwelling further on that.

Allison quickly and quietly searched the chamber from one end to the other, but found nothing. No clues left behind, no hints at all. Too clean for that. But near the back of the chamber, behind the altar, Allison discovered a very small door. It was unlocked, and indeed, had no lock of any kind on it. Even so, she barely managed to squeeze through the opening to the room beyond.

It was very small and ill-lit, with only the candles from the ritual chamber to light the storage room. Several crates stacked in a neat pile were full of dried food, mainly meat, and a barrel in the corner smelled strongly of alcohol. A close examination of the store room, around and under the various crates and barrels, revealed nothing. Allison searched again through the chamber.

As there was nothing else of note, Allison closely inspected the altar. It was granite, most likely, and had been used quite often for some ritual involving the use of fire. Soot clung so tightly to the surface that even her fingernail could not scrape it loose. Nothing about the materials it was made of or the design used in its construction amounted to a usable clue. Near the back of the alter, however, barely visible beneath the glossy sheen of the floor, Allison spotted faint scratches. Almost as if the altar had been moved.

Being very careful not to tip the altar over, Allison put her entire weight against the granite and pushed. For a moment, it resisted. But Allison pushed again and the stone finally shifted. It slid begrudgingly across the floor, thankfully not making much noise against the smooth marble. Once moved, the altar revealed a hidden chamber beneath the floor. Allison moved aside to allow in some of the flickering candlelight.

Clearly this was where they'd lit their fires, as the chamber was filled with soot and bits of burnt wood and other flammable materials. Without hesitation, Allison plunged her hand deep into the pile. After a few moments, her hand retreated, clutching a bundle of half-burnt documents. Someone had obviously meant to get rid of them, and very nearly succeeded. Many of the pages were blackened to the point where nothing was legible and many others had become so covered in clinging soot that no amount of work could ever make anything of them. In the dim light, she worked quickly, scouring one page and them moving on to the next.

Near the end, the pages were not quite so damaged. Even there the writing had begun to fade away, however, as the book had not been well taken care of, and she still struggled to make out what she was trying to read. Then at last, she found what appeared to be a list of names. Many were unknown to her, but two stood out. One had been crossed out, which was not uncommon among the others, but one was not. "Julia Ahbin," crossed out, and "Marcia Loren."

Allison brushed a bit more of the soot away and then stuffed the book deep into a pocket. She pushed the altar back into place, making sure that it looked as it had when she'd first arrived.

The house above was quiet and still, giving no indication that anyone was awake or aware that a trespasser was inside, but she'd already pressed her luck enough for one night. After gathering up the pieces of broken glass, Allison tossed them through the window and then climbed up after them. The frigid air from outside meant the broken window would quickly be found, but there was little she could do about that aside from press a large rock against the opening and hope that a servant got the blame.

Allison hurried back through the streets of Illdara, once again avoiding the pools of light that threatened to expose her. Back at the King's Crown, she entered through the servant's entrance around back. Thankfully, they never locked that door, as the inn stayed open well into the night. She moved quietly through the narrow halls, past the kitchen where servants still came and went with steins of drink and plates of food, and finally to the common room. No one saw her enter. At a table in the corner, she waited.

Just before midnight, Marcia Loren appeared in the common room. She went from table to table, taking orders and giving men deep in their drink a pretty face to help them forget their cares. She turned and saw Allison, who waved her over.

"Hello, Detective," Marcia said. "Could I get you something?"

Allison shook her head. "I'd like to talk with you instead. Preferably somewhere private."

"Private?" the girl asked, clearly confused. "Well, if you want, Detective. We can talk in the back room."

Once in the back room, Allison checked the hallway and then quietly shut the door. The two were alone.

"The Duganite cult," Allison said, "what do you know about them?"

"'What...do I know about them?'" The girl was already trembling. "They...I don't..."

"Marcia," Allison said, lightly touching the girl's arm, "you've been honest and open with me in the past, but this is of the utmost importance. If you know something, anything, then you *must* tell me."

Marcia's eyes darted about the room, refusing to meet Allison's, and her hands nervously worked. It was the conflict, her desire to be helpful and friendly against that ingrained suspiciousness and introversion.

"Marcia, please."

"Alright!" Marcia cried. "Alright, I'll tell you what I know." She took a deep, shuddering breath and then exhaled slowly. "They came to me, their people, and asked me to join. I'd heard of them before, everyone in Illdara has, but...but I'd never met anyone who said they were a member before and I only knew a little bit about what they believed."

"But you didn't join, did you?"

For a moment, Marcia was silent. "No," she said, nervously smoothing the front of her apron, "no, I didn't join. There was something about them, something that made me nervous and frightened just to be around them. They came to me twice at home and once here at the inn. Mr. Neal, the innkeeper, told them not to come here again, otherwise he'd make trouble with the police. I haven't seen them since. That was about nine months ago. Even so...even so, I've been afraid to leave the inn except during the day."

"Did they ever say why they wanted you to join?"

Marcia shook her head. "They never said why, but they were so persistent."

"Have you ever heard of someone named 'Julia Ahbin?'"

"No," said Marcia, "I've never heard of her before. Is she important to your case?"

"In a way. Thank you for answering my questions, Marcia, you were very helpful."

Marcia smiled. "Anything I can do to help, Detective."

Allison watched her disappear down the hallway. Maybe Inspector Jairyn was right about Julia Ahbin, maybe she had run away with a pocketful of her employer's coin. If that was truly the case, Allison finally knew why. She touched the copper ring shoved deep in a pocket. But maybe the inspector was wrong, so very wrong.

Tomorrow...tomorrow, she would twist Inspector Jairyn's arm until he let her take a detachment of officers to Faustus Prin's home to turn the place upside-down until they found the evidence she needed to put them all behind bars. Tomorrow.

Chapter 14

The back of Allison's head throbbed painfully. Her vision was unfocused, blurry, but she could see figures of different sizes and shapes moving back and forth in front of her. Cold water struck her face like a sharp slap. She gasped loudly, her mind recoiling from the sudden flood of sensations.

Men in dark robes and silvery masks stood around her, staring up at her, as she hung suspended above the floor. Their outlines bent and warped, as if shimmering from a great heat. Her arms and legs were tightly secured, making it impossible to move. She turned her head this way and that, but saw nothing save more of the cultists and her own limbs tied down to a flat slab of stone. The same slab of stone to which she'd seen the cult's sacrifice brought.

A dream.

A dream?

In an instant, she remembered returning to her room at the inn after talking with Marcia. She remembered going to sleep almost immediately. She remembered waking a short time later to muffled sounds that seemed far too close. She remembered a sharp smell, as of something burning. And that was all.

"Hello, Detective," one of the cultists said. Even without a face, Allison knew that it was Faustus Prin. "I'd hoped that our next meeting would not be in such a place, but you really did bring this upon yourself."

"What are you doing?!" Allison exclaimed.

"Only what we've done for centuries. It's an honor," he said quite calmly, "to be presented to Paragar as a sacrifice. You have nothing to fear, nothing at all." His left hand rose from under his robe, grasping a ceremonial dagger. Its blade was a wicked thing, twisted and curved like the tail of a serpent. From such a close proximity, she could see the serrated edges. Conley had said that the wounds were strange, uneven, as if they'd been made by a ceremonial dagger of some kind. The dagger rose higher, coming even with her heart. Allison was helpless, able only to wait for the inevitable.

"Faustus! Stop!" came a loud exclamation from the back of the chamber. Allison swiveled her head to see. Coming down the stone steps was Inspector Jairyn, his face as flat and emotionless as it always seemed to be. He walked over and looked up at her, one corner of his thin lips curled just slightly. She realized, then, what she should have realized some time ago.

"You've been helping them," she said, and the last sliver of hope she had slipped away.

He turned away from her without speaking.

"Surely you don't mean to let her go?" Faustus asked.

"Don't be foolish, she's seen and heard too much, as you said. But do you not find it a strange coincidence that she found her way so deeply into our world, a stranger who only just recently came to Illdara?"

The dagger disappeared back under Faustus's robe. "It was mere chance which brought her here, and her overbearing curiosity."

"No, I think not," the inspector said. "There is more to her than such a simple thing as chance. She has been brought to us, don't you see?

The last piece necessary to raise Paragar from his tomb, the living sacrifice. Everything about her perfectly fits the prophecies."

They both turned to her.

"Ah," said Faustus, a low sigh escaping through barely-parted lips. "Yes, I can see it now. It is as you said it would be, Inspector. All our work has not, then, been in vain." His voice grew louder. "Make the final preparations! Our time has now come!"

The cultists moved in a blur all around her, setting up arrays of burning candles, stone altars draped with sea-blue material, carved idols, and other implements important to their ceremonies. Soon, they began to sing in a low chant, a song ethereal yet somehow almost savage, as well. Their voices echoed through the chamber and Allison saw that the water in the pool behind her boiled and raged.

Their song quickly reached a fever pitch. They threw their heads back, staring towards the ceiling through the tiny holes in their frightening masks. The lights danced and played across the polished metal and it looked as though the engraved shapes, of men and beasts from the sea, moved in tune with the song in a grotesque dance.

The smoke from the candles they'd placed around the slab of stone burned Allison's nostrils and then clawed its way down her throat. They'd put something in the tallow, some drug. Her vision became blurry again, her mind sluggish. The dancing cultists seemed caught in molasses as their movements slowed and became more exaggerated. The dull pounding of a drum somewhere in the distance coursed through every inch of her body, until she shuddered and trembled with each beat.

Water exploded up from the pool and cascaded all around them. In the dim light at the back of the chamber, Allison thought she could see a shape emerge. But it was too big, too unnatural. The chanting continued, faster and faster.

"Come now, Paragar!" Faustus cried, his body writhing in religious ecstasy. "Come now and receive our final sacrifice to you! Come now into our world! Break loose your surly bonds and return to this mortal world! Come now, Paragar!"

The shape slowly emerged from the pool. It towered above them all, tentacles and other bizarre appendages flailing in the air as its gaping maw, ringed with glistening teeth, grew ever wider. A single eye, as black as midnight and as large as a barrel, stared back at her, blind but still seeing, and she saw in it depths of cruelty and hatred that were impossible to imagine.

Allison would have screamed if there'd been any breath at all in her lungs with which to scream. All the detective work she'd done, all the clues she'd found and examined, would come to naught. But they'd always been for naught, in the face of this unnatural, otherworldly abomination. No power of man could hope to combat such a thing, no murder or string of murders could ever matter where this creature, this Paragar, was concerned. This was the true secret of Illdara.

Yet in the back of her mind, she wondered. A living sacrifice, that's what they'd kept saying. Why should it matter if she were alive or dead, Paragar would devour her just the same. And then it struck her. As the tentacles of that horrible monstrosity slid through the air, inching closer, she knew what it was that would make her different from the other sacrifices. Paragar did not intend to consumer her. Allison found her breath at last and screamed.

"My lord!" came a startled cry. "My lord!"

A young man came running down the stone steps, his face pale and his breathing labored. His appearance broke the spell and Paragar sank back beneath the waves. Allison felt her entire body go limp.

Faustus turned to face the young man. "What is it, you fool?!" he snapped. "You've ruined the ceremony! You've ruined everything!"

"I'm sorry, my lord, I'm sorry!" the young man babbled, bowing so low that he nearly bent himself in half. "Bu-but there's been another murder in the city!"

Inspector Jairyn was in front of the young man in an instant, grasping him by the collar. "Another murder?! Who?!"

"Ye-yes, Chief Inspector, a sailor. We found him less than half an hour ago. Oh, you must come quickly, Chief Inspector, you must!"

In all the sudden commotion, everyone had forgotten about Allison. In a bout of desperation, she struggled against the bonds that held her wrists, pulling and tugging with what strength she could muster. But the knots had been done up tight, by an expert hand.

Something flashed through the air, striking the rope that held her left hand and then skittering off into the darkness. The rope fell away. A knife from her boot quickly cut loose her other arm and then her feet. She dropped to the floor, less than a step from where her pistol lay, discarded and forgotten. They'd waited until the end to take it away from her. She snatched it up and ran.

A passage led away from the chamber, pitch-black. With no time to stop and search for a lantern or torch, she plunged into the darkness with her hands held before her, feeling along the walls. Even so, there could be sudden drops into bottomless chasms or even simply steps going down to a lower level that would be more than enough to shatter one of her legs, or her neck. But the cries of the cultists came after her, men and women who likely knew the layout of the underground far better than she. And so Allison ran.

Down in that abyss where there was no sense of time or place, no sense of direction. Only the darkness, as deep as darkness had ever been, and the cries and yells, the stamping of boots, seeming to come from all around her; only the fear that surged through her mind, of being caught and returned to that chamber. Allison stumbled as the ground disappeared from under her feet and she pitched forward, falling through the darkness. Falling and falling.

Her arms hit first, held in front of her body for some small measure of protection. Then her chest. Air rushed from her lungs. She slid across the slick stones. For several seconds, she lay on the ground, too stunned to stand. As she finally raised her eyes, she could see the moon hanging low in the sky, reflecting perfectly off the icy sea. The roiling waters had almost frozen solid, especially a thin strip between the northern arm of the peninsula and Ellsberth Island.

Nothing to her left or right but the sheer cliffs, hundreds of feet high, and the ice-choked bay surrounding them. To swim those waters was a death sentence, to go back the way she'd come was worse than a death sentence. Ellsberth Island was her only option, more than a mile away across a narrow bridge of ice. Only a fool would take that chance, only a desperate, frightened fool.

The ice cracked and moaned beneath her weight as she carefully walked out onto it, hesitantly, slowly. No other sounds reached her ears, not even a breath of wind or the pounding of the surf against rocky cliffs. The ocean slowly undulated up and down, rhythmic and hypnotic, as the great chunks of ice calmed the raging seas. The island ahead was silent, dark and dead, save for where the beam from the lighthouse, still turning in a lazy circle, gently caressed it every half-minute.

The island was closer to the northern arm than any other part of the city, but the distance was still a full mile. A full mile across a frozen sea that might give way beneath her at any time and make this flight a futile gesture. Yet she continued on, even as the city fell away behind her and the great blackness of the island loomed ever larger before her.

The air was cold, so very cold, worse than any winter night she could remember back at the capital, and it sliced through her frock, waistcoat, and shirt as if she were wearing nothing at all. The warmth of her body, the sweat of exertion and fear, left her half-soaked and half-frozen.

Allison looked behind her several times, to see if her pursuers might be coming across the ice bridge after her, but saw nothing except the moonlit ice and the sheer cliffs. No one in their right mind would venture out across the ice.

At last, the cold air seemed to burn away the lingering effects of the candle smoke, enough to help keep her focused on what she was doing, but soon it made her mind and body grow numb. Even so, the images of that...creature...remained. They chilled her bones more than the air ever could. Seeing what she'd seen was enough to make her want to curl up on the ground and sob. But if she was the only thing to stand between the world and the Duganite's 'god,' then it was all the more reason to flee as far from them as possible.

The moon rose ever higher, but Allison did not stop.

About an hour past midnight, her feet finally touched solid ground again. The island was fairly large, with the eastern half covered in a thick pine forest. In the silvery moonlight, she could see a simple dock off in the distance, sheltered by a narrow cove. The western half of the island was covered by a steep hill, upon which stood the Pembrook Asylum. Supposedly, the asylum had not seen use in a number of decades.

The forested half of the island was thick with trees and undergrowth. Long, fat roots curled up through the soil, ever threatening to throw her on the ground; low-hanging limbs slapped and scratched at her face and arms.

Allison finally emerged from the forest and came to a narrow, gravel road that led from the docks up to the asylum complex. In the dim light, it was impossible to tell whether the deep ruts, parallel and narrow, had been made long ago or were a more recent addition. She followed them up the hill.

The asylum was surrounded by a rock wall, nine feet high and crowned with pointed, metal spikes, which more dangerous now than when they were new, thanks to the jagged edges brought about by a thick layer of rust. Attempting to climb over would be no fun exercise, that much was certain. The gate itself was equally imposing, built from thick, wrought iron bars and sealed with stout chains from top to bottom. Only a battering ram would be able to get through all that.

Allison searched the wall all around the asylum, looking for any signs of weakness in the wall itself or for any locations where the metal spears had come loose and fallen away. Two hours past midnight, when Allison was almost ready to give up entirely and find somewhere out of the way to hide in, she found a narrow gap between the wall and the ground. It was more animal hole than secret entrance, but she was given little else in the way of a choice. She dug away dirt and leaves and then flattened her body against the ground.

The bottom of the wall pressed down on her from above and the hard-packed soil pressed from below as she carefully squeezed through the opening. Tighter and tighter. It was as though the wall were slowly crushing her, pushing the air from her lungs, pushing her further into the ground, as her fingers dug into the dirt on the other side. Tighter and tighter.

With one final pull, she slid through the opening and came to the other side. Free of that awful vice, she breathed deeply. The air was so cold that it burned her lungs. Allison realized that her hands and feet had stopping tingling and were beginning to feel very numb. Frostbite. She plunged her hands deep into her pockets and hurried to the nearest entrance to the asylum.

The buildings were old, nearly as old as the city itself. Her briefing back at the capital had mentioned the island in passing, and the asylum itself in even less detail, but had stated that the asylum had once been a thriving medical facility that treated afflictions even beyond those of the mind. This period wasn't to last and soon the facility lay empty and abandoned, for reasons not even guessed at. And that was the extent of what she knew. Given how dark and dilapidated it all was, Allison was inclined to believe what she'd read.

One of the larger buildings had a pair of doors near where she'd climbed under the wall. They were, of course, quite locked. Allison briefly considered kicking them down, but decided to check the nearby windows first. They were all locked, as well, but also were covered by a mesh of thick, metal bars to further deter entrance. Allison returned to the door and plunged her knife into the gap between door and wall. Her fingers, completely numb, were almost of no use at all, but she'd done this enough times that the actions came quickly and with no wasted time. The lock finally clicked. Allison opened the door and went inside.

It was almost impossible to see anything, away from the moonlight. Allison stumbled her way through the building, looking for some interior room. Along one hallway were strung about a dozen lanterns, many of which had rusted away to nothing. A few of them had not, but many of those were dry and not even the smell of oil remained. But one near the end sloshed faintly when she grabbed it. The oil was thick and black, more tar than anything else, but it would do.

With some luck, and little effort, she finally found an interior room. With the door shut tight and no windows to give away her location, Allison produced a packet of matches. The moist air of the underground and then of the icy sea had ruined them. They were now nothing more than sad, little bits of limp paper. No matter how hard she tried, they would not catch fire. If only she had some of the matches the killer had left with Mrs. Celeste. Finally, she threw the packet away and then felt along the floor for a rock or bit of stone.

Once she'd found a suitable candidate, she slashed her knife across its jagged surface. Sparks sputtered, dancing on the wick like stars in the night sky. But they didn't catch. She tried again. Nothing. Again. Nothing. Barely able to choke back the sobs that formed deep in her chest, she frantically slashed at the rock as its sharp edges dug into her palm. Finally, the sparks caught. The lantern flared, light exploded through the darkness.

Allison's eyes burned as she held them half-shut. It was like staring directly at the sun.

For a long time, she sat with her hands clamped down around the glass bulb. She wondered if the cultists were still after her, she wondered if Inspector Jairyn had cooked up some story to send his men out after her, she wondered how things were going with the third murder, and she wondered whether she could survive the rest of the night in such a bitter cold.

Even inside, with a roof and four walls, the cold seeped through her frock, to the thin shirt beneath, and all the way through her skin to turn her bones to ice. No food, no water. No bed, no fire. She was almost amazed at how quickly her situation had turned. Not so long ago, she'd nearly driven herself insane for want to be away from the King's Crown Inn. But now...now, she wanted nothing more than to be back there, to hide beneath those thick, warm blankets and think of nothing but a good night's sleep.

It was something worth crying over, but the tears would only freeze to her face, or freeze before they even fell, and simply make her feel all the worse for it. Allison let her eyes wander about the room, looking, but not really looking *for* anything. It appeared to be a storage room of some kind, piled high in one corner with rotting crates. If they'd ever contained anything, the contents were long gone. Dust lay thick on the floor, undisturbed except for where Allison herself had walked.

A fire would certainly go a long way, and there was enough material nearby to keep one going for a long time, but the smoke would, no doubt, be visible in the moonlight and make it abundantly clear where she'd fled to. A calculated risk, freezing to death, perhaps, or being captured. But a small fire, with the smoke allowed to dissipate throughout the asylum first, might keep her presence a secret.

Allison cleared a spot in the middle of the room and piled up some chunks of wood from the crates in the corner. Being very careful with the lantern, she lightly touched the dried wood with the flaming wick. The fire spread quickly, pushing back at Illdara's winter cold. She sat crouched over the small fire for some time, soaking in the warmth and letting it melt away the block of ice that her body had become. And she waited.

Chapter 15

The asylum was doubly cold and doubly dark away from even such a small fire. Allison kept her lantern with her, the wick as low as it would go and still burn. It gave off little light to see by, but even that faint light was a great comfort.

Dilapidated rooms, piled high with old medical equipment and tools or entirely empty. Long, narrow hallows choked with unidentifiable debris. The dust of decades, thick on every surface, cobwebs hanging like drapery from nearly every corner. And there was rust and rot in equal measures throughout, all giving clear evidence of ill-use.

It was strange to think that she might be the first person to walk those halls in decades. Stranger still to think of all those who had lived and died so long ago in this place. Allison was not one to give credence to tales of ghosts and spirits, but this was certainly the place where such things would be found if they *did* exist.

What she did not find, however, were documents or correspondence of any kind. She wasn't entirely sure what they would reveal to her if she found any, but there was always the faint hope that a search in this old institution might reveal some shred of evidence, some clue, that would lead her back to the murders in the city or to the Duganite cult and their rituals. But she didn't even know herself what good such a shred of evidence might do, even if she could find it. She continued through a deeply-ingrained set of motions, not allowing herself to give in to doubt and despair.

Her search dragged on through the early morning hours. Empty rooms, empty hallways, finding nothing but the decay of an isolated world slowly returning from whence it came. With the realization that her search was becoming more futile, Allison became all the more frantic. She began to run from one room to the next, her head twisting this way and that as she tried to take in each new area as quickly as possible.

There must be something in that old asylum. There must be! Yet she could find nothing at all. Her search would prove futile, her flight across the icy bridge would prove futile. She would be forced to return to the city with nothing she could use for leverage. Whoever found her first would immediately hand her over to Inspector Jairyn and Faustus. Even the King's Crown wouldn't be safe.

The fear she felt was her father's fear, as the case he was working on deepened. He knew that he was going to die, it was only a matter of when that fatal shot, that fatal knife to the heart, finally came. Yet he'd not given up, and it would have been so easy for him to do so.

His fellow officers, his bosses, they'd all warned him to give up. They'd even come to Allison, in their own subtle way, to have her convince her father to give up. But she'd said nothing to him about it, and he was too much of a police officer to let the matter go. And when he died, his friends turned away. It had just been a random act, no need to dig too deeply. They knew, they all knew. The desperate pleas of a girl who'd just lost everything had gone unanswered.

And so, Allison continued in her search, because she was her father's daughter.

With morning coming soon, Allison finally came across what she'd been searching for. Most of the doors that she'd seen had been unlocked, a few were even entirely off their hinges. But in an isolated corner of one building, Allison found a door that not only was locked, but locked very, very well. Two bolts were set into the wall and the door even had an iron gate pulled in front of it, further denying entrance. If there was anything to be found, it would be beyond that door.

Allison produced her knife and a long, thin wire, thanking the gods that she'd seen the value in taking that lock-picking course back at the academy. Her hands were not quite so frozen as before, so she worked slowly and carefully, probing each lock with the wire and pressing against each bolt with her knife. It was slow work, meticulous work.

An hour before dawn, the final lock came loose. Allison slowly pushed the door open. A desk, low and ordinary with no adornments; a cabinet in the corner, two drawers; and absolutely nothing else. She opened each drawer of the cabinet first, but found them both empty. There was not even a single shred of paper in either of them. The desk had no drawers at all. For a moment, Allison stood in the middle of the room and stared. It made no sense.

But as she stared, her eyes fixed on the wall. Something wasn't quite right, the wall almost appeared to be crooked. With haste, Allison slid her hands all along the four walls, feeling for anything irregular. Finding nothing, she searched the floor. At last, she found a tiny switch hidden beneath the desk.

When pressed, a part of the wall slid back into a recess, revealing narrow steps that descended below the foundation. More steps. More steps into some dark abyss where anything at all might be lurking. Allison sighed, long and low. Her room at the King's Crown Inn, just for an hour or two. Just for half an hour. She'd almost be willing to give up on the whole affair just for that. Yet her detective instincts wouldn't let her, not while the mystery was still unsolved, not while there was one more dark hole to crawl through in search of some elusive clue. Even if all else failed her, Allison knew those instincts would not.

The steps went down below the foundation of the asylum, to a broad hallway that continued on past the ring of light from Allison's lantern. A doorway on her right opened into a small room, a guardhouse of sorts, which was occupied. The guard's hat was pulled low over his face, his chest silently rose and fell. Without hesitation, Allison approached the man from behind and caught him just below the base of his skull with the butt of her pistol. The man uttered a faint cry as he fell. Unconscious, not dead. She checked his pockets, but found only a few coins and a long knife stuffed down in his boot. The room was otherwise empty.

The long hallway led to more rooms, all of which were more tightly secured than her skills with a lockpick could overcome. Many of the locks appeared so rusted that even the proper key might not be enough to gain entrance. In the meager light of her lantern, it was hard to see just what, if anything, was in those three rooms. She raised her lantern high and peered through the bars set into one of the doors. Piles of old rags, mostly, nothing that immediately caught her attention. Aside from the guard, nothing else was down there, certainly nothing to indicate why his presence was necessary. Maybe just a nightwatchman, just someone to watch over the place to make sure that everything at the abandoned asylum was quiet. He wouldn't be in any condition to answer her many questions for quiet a while.

Annoyed with herself and frustrated at the lack of finding anything at the asylum, even in the one location most likely to contain some valuable piece of information, Allison turned away from the door. But something stopped her. She turned back to the door, raising the light in the lantern and peering again through the bars. One of the piles moved.

Her eyes widened as she stared. The piles of rags came into focus at last, revealing their true nature. The room was filled with people. Homeless people, by the looks of them. They'd been so quiet and so still when she'd looked the first time, and their clothes were so ragged and dirty, that she'd almost overlooked them entirely. Allison's heart hammered against the walls of her chest. More sacrifices for Paragar? She looked back towards the guards station, towards the stairs, expecting the Duganites to suddenly appear. But the basement was silent, even the homeless in those cells didn't make a sound. Allison breathed.

"Are you alright?" she whispered.

But the homeless didn't respond. Except for a few subtle hints, the twitching of muscles and the faint movements from breathing, they barely looked alive.

"Can you hear me?" Allison called, taking a chance by raising her voice.

One of the homeless looked up, a young woman whose face was horribly scarred. She looked towards the light with dull disinterest. Her pupils were narrow and listless, looking without seeing. Allison had seen the same look on the sacrifice brought to the Duganite ceremony. They were all heavily drugged. The woman laid her head back down, her eyes still open.

Allison grasped one of the doors and pulled. The locks rattled, but held firm. Her pistol might knock one of the locks loose--might--but she didn't have any extra powder or balls for a second shot. And she couldn't risk the ball ricocheting into one of the rooms and injuring someone. They were trapped and she had no means to free them.

Allison's eyes darted around the hallway, searching, searching. A key, a crowbar, a large rock, anything which she might use to open those doors. Nothing. Then she spied, low to the floor, a small drain whose metal grate was missing. It was all dried up, and had been for some time. With nothing else that she could think to do, Allison bent down and reached into the drain. Her hands felt cold metal. Her fingers closed around what felt like a box and then pulled it out. Small, metal, held shut by a tiny lock.

Allison stuck her knife inside the lock's loop and twisted. At first, it resisted, but Allison was desperate for an answer. Finally, the lock gave way and the box was soon open. Documents, about a dozen in all, folded once and then crammed down into the metal box. She read through them all, eyes darting from one line to the next. They were receiving papers, documenting the coming and going of cargo. Line after line of names and more names. Hundreds. Dates for receiving, dates for delivery. Even the names of ships. One name on the documents was a name Allison knew: Julia Ahbin. Delivered. Received.

"Gods," Allison exclaimed under her breath.

She looked up and saw the room full of drugged homeless. She looked down and saw the list of names. The pieces of the puzzle slid together, the image became clear.

The abandoned buildings, the food delivered to the homeless, the disappearances, the paranoia, all of it. Slavery...human lives sold and bartered. The police, the cult, maybe even the local government itself...how deeply did this conspiracy go? A shudder ran along her spine as she tried to imagine the scope of this horrible trade. The pages had so many names, more than she could count, and this seemed only to cover a few years' time. Victoria Celeste...had she dug too deeply and been killed for her curiosity?

Allison's mind worked as she considered the possibility. It may have been true that Mrs. Celeste had found something, or was very close to finding something, but surely killing her in the city would only draw even more attention to their activities. No, something wasn't quite right about that. Ambushing her in the hills, dumping her body out at sea. Those would obfuscate the matter far better. And the old beggar? And the third killing? To say nothing of the clues, which almost seemed to be showing her the way.

Allison quickly stuffed the documents into one of her pockets and climbed back up out of the pit. She hurried through the asylum, looking for the way out. Someone had to be told, someone that she could trust with such information. But who in Illdara could she trust?

In a long hallway that led to the building's main entrance, Allison stopped. Slowly, she turned. The hall behind her was completely empty, but she was certain that she'd sensed some faint movement.

"You're so close now."

The voice was low, faintly heard.

Allison closed her fingers around the hilt of her pistol. "You led me here, didn't you?"

"Clever girl, very clever. You'd not have found it all on your own, no one would have. This was the only way."

"You murdered three people to bring me here? To expose what was really going on in Illdara? It was all for *this*?"

There was pause, a very long pause, and Allison thought that the voice had gone.

"Yes."

"Do you think the ends justify your acts?!" Allison shouted defiantly, angrily. Her voice echoed over and over.

"I don't expect you to approve, Detective. In fact, I'd be disappointed if you did. This simply is how it must be."

"Give yourself up, come with me back to the city. I'll sort this all out somehow and take you back with me to the capital. The king will deal with Illdara and its vile trade. And make sure no one else is sacrificed to that...*thing*."

A brief chuckle, dry. "Quite a show they put on for you, anyone in your position would have believed it was truly real. Especially after they spent so much effort building it up in your mind."

"A show?"

"Paragar...nothing more than a wooden skeleton wrapped in canvas, operated by levers and pulleys. But real enough in such a dark hole filled with that awful smoke."

So many more things made sense. The whole case had been a battleground, a conflict between the murderer and the city of Illdara. The wild, whispered tales, the mysterious cult, the clues and hints. The murderer had been leading her to the truth and the cult had been carefully leading her astray.

"Why?" Allison asked. "Why would they do that?"

"How much easier to hide the truth if the detective sent from the capital returned raving of risen gods and secret sacrifices, her mind broken and her body left as little more than an empty shell? Spring would be a

156

long time coming; plenty of time for people to forget, for the truth to be obscured, and the matter settled. And they very nearly succeeded."

Allison felt sick at her stomach, sick at being nothing more than a pawn for either side. "Come with me," she said at last, "help me bring all this to light. I'll make sure they know how you helped me."

A long pause, and Allison almost thought the killer was going to accept her offer.

"I can't," the killer said at last.

"Then I'll take this city apart to find you and bring you to justice," Allison said. "I swear it."

"You won't have to take the city apart, Detective, the people are already very close to doing that themselves."

"What?"

"The third victim, a sailor. I left a memento at the scene for his friends to find. A gold lapel, exactly like the one that Inspector Jairyn lost three weeks ago."

And then the killer was gone.

Chapter 16

Allison could spend a solid week searching every inch of the asylum and still find no trace of the killer. If what he said of the third murder was true, and she had no reason to disbelieve it, there'd be nothing left of Illdara after that week was out. Riots in other cities could be controlled and eventually contained. A riot in Illdara, as isolated and confined as the city was, would be a dreadful thing to see. Instead of a futile search, Allison hurried down to the dock as the sky behind the mountains to the east began to turn a dark shade of purple.

Aside from a rickety dock just barely wide enough to accommodate anything larger than a small schooner, and unlikely to hold much more weight than one or two people at a time, there was only a rundown guardhouse. It was locked up, but Allison made quick work of the locks and then searched the interior. Someone had shoved a small boat--really just a one-man canoe--into one of the corners behind a coat-rack covered in rotting coats. A few experimental raps with her knuckle against the hull did not fill her with confidence, but that was all she was given to work with.

Dragging the canoe in one hand and carrying a broken-off floor plank in the other, Allison hurried down to the dock. The canoe settled into the water and appeared buoyant enough, so she eased down into it, being careful not to let one side or the other dip too far into the icy water. Through some miracle, it managed to float.

As the sky brightened, she could see smoke rising from Illdara. Not from fireplaces or the alleys where the homeless lived, for there was far too much and it was far too concentrated. The rioting had already begun.

Though the waves were not so great, the bay grew thicker and thicker with great chunks of ice that bumped and battered the tiny vessel as it moved further from the dock. Allison did her best to push them aside when they came too close, but many of them were simply too big and too heavy. And there were just too many of them. Each hit elicited the sharp crack of splintering wood. With the floor plank in hand, she paddled as hard as she could.

Halfway to the city, about a mile out from the island, the canoe began to leak. It was only a small trickle at first, but that wouldn't hold true for long. The hull had been compromised and the trickle would soon become a flow. With sweat pouring down her face despite the sub-freezing temperature, Allison paddled all the harder.

With the docks and all their ships coming into view, the canoe was nearly half-full of freezing sea-water. Her legs were growing numb and her boots were quickly turning into blocks of ice. Allison continued to paddle, straining against tired muscles that begged for rest. Finally, the dock was in reach. She grabbed one of the sturdy beams.

A chunk of ice struck the hull with a great crash. Water flooded the canoe. Her fingers closed on the beam and she pulled herself up as the canoe fell away, sinking into the black waters. With great effort, she pulled herself higher up the wooden framework and onto solid ground, or a close approximation of it. She lay for a moment, sprawled on the cold wood, desperately trying to catch her breath. Two miles through snow-choked sea was not a thing lightly done, but she had not the time for proper rest.

A few overturned carts burned unattended on Dagal Road as Allison hurried east towards Main, and several stores had had their windows broken and their doors torn from the hinges, but most of the activities appeared to have already moved deeper into the city. A trail of debris and fire led the way through the empty streets.

Allison followed it all the way to police headquarters. A large band of burly sailors, some two-hundred strong, many waving torches and various implements that they intended to use as makeshift cudgels, had surrounded the front of the structure and appeared to be very close to making an attempt at breaking down the front door. They were currently being held at bay by just a few officers.

Getting through the crowd wasn't difficult, as none of them even seemed to notice her because of their preoccupation. Finally, Allison pushed through to the front of the crowd. Several ship captains were arguing quite heatedly with one of the officers, who Allison was shocked to recognize as Constable Wilminson. Despite their argument, he turned to greet her.

"Deetective," he said with a crisp salute. Nothing about the man suggested that the situation bothered him in the slightest.

"Where is Inspector Jairyn?" Allison asked, raising her voice to be heard above the noise. The ship captains had ceased in their arguing and now turned their attention to her, as well.

"He was he-ah a few hours ago, but I've naught seen 'im since ahl this business stahted."

Allison turned to the captains. "Where's the body of the sailor?" she asked. "Was he brought to the coroner?"

The three appeared indignant at being addressed, especially by a woman who barely came to their shoulders.

"I don't see that that's any of your business, girl!" one of them growled. The others nodded their agreement.

"If you want to tear yourselves apart, that's your business," Allison growled back at them, too exhausted and scared and frustrated to even bother being polite, "but there's been murder committed here and I intend to have someone brought back to the capital to be hanged! If you impede my investigation at all, I'll assume it's because you've something to hide. Don't think that I won't have the king's army here at first thaw to turn this city upside down looking for the answers I need. That'll include what's left of your ships, if anything."

Her words seemed to make them all the more enraged. One of them, the biggest of the three, cocked his fist back and the implications of the action were clear. But before he could even begin to move his arm forward, a massive fist came from out of nowhere and slugged him across the jaw with blinding speed. The ship captain fell back against the sailors standing behind him. Constable Wilminson loomed over the three captains, his hand already back at his side. The man who'd been cuffed lurched forward, but was grabbed from behind by one of the other captains, who whispered something in his ear. They spoke briefly, heatedly.

"You're from the capital, right?" the captain asked, rubbing at his bruised jaw.

"That's right."

"You've got all of today," he said, and it was clear he didn't like giving her even that meager amount of time. "If you can't bring us something that'll convince us to back down by then, we'll break this door down and find the answers ourselves."

They did not, however, return to their ships as Allison had hoped they would. Rather, they simply stayed exactly where they were, pressed up against police headquarters. The torches were extinguished, so that was something. Allison followed Constable Wilminson inside.

"Ugly business," the constable said. "I'd arrest the laht of them if I 'ad enough men and cells."

"Was the body brought here?" Allison asked.

"It was, Deetective. Conley ought to be poking abowt on the poor chappie just now."

"Thank you, Constable. For everything."

"My pleasuah, Deetective. Aye'll do what I can with this rowdy laht, maybe 'twixt the two of us we kin keep tha city togethah."

Allison hurried to the morgue.

The body of the sailor was up on slab and Conley was in the process of inspecting various wounds, of which there were many. He didn't look up as she came in, though his assistants did.

"Is it the same as the others?"

"Same?" Conley asked, his face momentarily blank with incomprehension. "Ah yes, same. Many wounds, made from jagged knife, similar to others."

"What of the man himself?"

"Albert Kinnison," he said. "Several came forward earlier to say so. Sailor, early-twenties, worked as cargo clerk for merchant in port."

"Any signs of the rotting disease?"

"Rotting disease? Hmm...no obvious signs here, but possible he was in early stages."

Allison leaned back against the wall. "Could there be any other disease or ailment he might have been dying of? Or did our man go out of his way to send a message?"

Conley thought about this for a moment. "Nothing in chest cavity to indicate imminent death." He looked up at her through his thick glasses. "I will search cranial cavity now, will you wait?"

Allison nodded.

Conley produced a large bone-saw and then began to carefully slice away the flesh and bone that kept him from the dead man's brain. The work was slow and Allison chaffed at having to wait on a bit of evidence that likely would have little bearing on the case. But for reasons she struggled to understand, she *had* to know whether the man had a terminal disease or not.

Thirty minutes of work finally did the trick. Conley pulled away the top of the skull to reveal the brain beneath.

"Ah."

"What is it?" Allison asked.

"A growth," he said, "attached to brain, nearly size of silver coin. Very dangerous, no cure."

"This man didn't have long to live, did he?"

"No," Conley said, shaking his head. "A year, at most. Death was inevitable, painful."

"Did you find anything in any of the wounds?"

Conley fished around in a pocket of his apron and produced a small key.

"What does this unlock?" Allison asked.

"Your job, Detective, not mine."

The coroner turned back to his work, as one of the boys wrote on a sheet of parchment and the other continued to draw various pictures of the victim.

In the main building of police headquarters, the officers, armed with clubs and even a few pistols, had set up a makeshift barricade with several of their desks, as if they expected the front door to come crashing open at any moment. With Constable Wilminson and his men still outside, that seemed unlikely. But given the current mood in the city, it was far from impossible. No one tried to stop her as she went back to Inspector Jairyn's office in the corner of the room, nor when she opened the door and went inside.

The office looked much the same as when she'd last seen it, overflowing with case files and reports, all vying for attention on the limited space offered by the inspector's desk. He might have taken something with him when he left, but it was impossible to tell.

Allison moved stacks of papers and furniture, inspected as much of the floor and the walls as she could, but found nothing. No secret switches, no secret compartments to keep hidden some vital clue. The small office was too much of a mess to make a proper inspection, certainly not in the limited amount of time she'd been afforded. Allison halfheartedly picked up a stack of bulging folders and attempted to move them, when she accidentally bumped the large broadsword resting in the corner. With her hands full, it was impossible to catch it. The weapon fell with a loud clatter, its tip scraping across the tiles.

Allison set down the folders and bent to pick up the weapon. She stopped. The tile that the sword had been resting on was crooked. She picked it up and moved it aside, revealing a safe set into the foundation. It was small, with enough space for some documents and not much else. Here were the inspector's secrets, but picking this lock would be impossible.

A sudden thought came to Allison and she took the key from her pocket. Small and nondescript, no markings, probably copper, and that was all there was to say. Aside from a bit of blood smudged on it, the key looked new. If the killer could have gotten one of Inspector Jairyn's lapel buttons, he might also have taken the key to his hidden safe and had a copy made of it. The key slid into the lock. It turned. The door of the safe opened on its own.

As Allison had thought, the safe was full of documents. A quick glance of the contents indicated that none were particularly incriminating, merely personal in nature. The documents discussing the inspector's dealing with the slave trade likely had already been taken, if they existed. Many of the documents appeared out of order, others were ruffled or torn, as if someone had hastily pawed through them looking for certain ones. At the bottom of the safe was a document folded over several times. Allison plucked it out and unfolded it. A map.

The general outline appeared to be that of Illdara, but none of the roads or paths looked familiar. As Allison studied the map, she realized that it wasn't roads she was looking at, but the underground network of tunnels and passages. At the eastern edge of the southern arm was a marking of some kind, but it had faded so badly that she couldn't tell whether it was supposed to be a word or some kind of symbol. The underground meeting place for the Duganite cult was similarly marked. If Inspector Jairyn had fled, perhaps something was there in that second location that he was fleeing to. Allison tucked the parchment into a pocket of her frock and left police headquarters.

A metal lid, similar to the one Allison had found earlier, led down into the underground not far from the spot marked on the map. Once again, she crawled through narrow passages, trying to avoid getting covered in the noxious liquid that still ran freely down below the streets. This time, there was no guess work or intuition, only the map in one hand and the lantern in the other, leading her on towards where she hoped to find Inspector Jairyn. She didn't need to be careful, she only needed to hurry.

At last, the final hurdle appeared less than twenty feet from the cliff: a metal door. When locked, it would be impossible to pick or break down. At present, it was standing slightly ajar, with a bit of faint light creeping out through the opening. Allison's hand went to her flintlock pistol and she drew it. Her other hand rested lightly on the door. She breathed in. She breathed out.

In one quick movement, she flung the door to one side and burst through the opening, her pistol leading the way. Inspector Jairyn was lying on the floor, surrounded by a pool of blood. His throat had been slashed ear to ear. Behind him was a vine of royal thane growing up one wall, thriving even in that near-darkness where it was only just above freezing. Some of the flower's purple petals had fallen to the floor, unnoticed. A shadow in the far corner moved. The room had another exit.

Allison ran after the shadow as it fled along a passage parallel to the sea. Then it disappeared around a corner. By the time Allison got there, the shadow was gone, escaped behind another metal door, this one shut and firmly locked. But she knew who it was, it was the same man who'd killed thrice already. Whatever reason had possessed him to come to Illdara and play out this twisted game, it was all over now. A small boat, manned by a lone figure, receded out across the ice-choked sea.

She returned to the tiny room, seeing again the chief inspector, still lying sprawled on the floor. He was dead and the truth had at last come to light. When spring came, the king's army would march through the mountain pass and finally put an end to Illdara's vile trade. Yet it was a hollow victory.

Chapter 17

With the recovery of Chief Inspector Jairyn's body, the crowd of sailors dispersed. The three captains remained behind, along with several guards, to make sure that their voices continued to be heard.

Faustus Prin's estate was found sealed up tight and the first police officer on the scene received a lead ball through his leg from a second story window. Barricades were erected and all entrances watched day and night. After several days, the estate burned to the ground. Faustus Prin was never found, dead or alive.

Garrus Locklain was arrested on his ship, having never left his quarters despite the discovery of the third murder, the riots, and the uncovering of the slave trade. No evidence was found to implicate him, but he remained confined to his ship and was stripped of his title as winter harbormaster.

The houses of Illdara's three wealthy families, those visited by Victoria Celeste, were raided and all those who lived there were taken into custody. They were questioned over the course of several days and much more time was spent poring over every last bit of evidence taken from each, but no link was ever found. Inspector Jairyn's revelation that Blake Timsley had been found dead was proven to be a lie. His disappearance remained a mystery throughout the winter months.

In the end, Allison informed the people of the city, and the sailors, that Chief Inspector Jairyn had been behind the whole affair, attempting to throw suspicion away from the slave trade by setting up a series of bizarre killings. His lapel being left behind had been an accident, just a little twist of fate that caused all his plans to unravel. He'd taken his own life rather than face judgment. It rang hollow in her ears, but they'd never have accepted the truth.

The homeless on Ellsberth Island, hidden beneath the asylum, were quietly freed once the situation in the city was finally under control. Constable Wilminson went personally, taking only a few of his most trusted officers. Allison told them little, only that they'd been kidnapped for the Duganites as part of some ceremony. The constable accepted this without question. The homeless could remember nothing of how they'd gotten to the island.

Several days passed before the panic and confusion subsided. Allison returned at last to the King's Crown, finally finding a moment's respite. She could count on her hands the number of hours she'd slept during that time, sitting in a chair at police headquarters.

"Who would have thought that Inspector Jairyn could have been behind such terrible things?" Marcia asked as she brought out Allison's dinner. "I always did think he was a bit cold, but a murderer?" She shook her head in disbelief.

"Appearances are not always the full truth," Allison said, helping herself to a thick slab of steak smothered in gravy.

"Well, everyone agrees that he did it and the evidence you found certainly points that way. Nobody can say otherwise, can they?"

"No, I suppose not."

"It's good to see this business over with," Marcia said. "I could hardly sleep at night thinking about somebody creeping into my room and..." She trailed off as a shiver ran the length of her body. "Anyway, it's all over now. If there's anything you need, Detective, anything at all, don't hesitate to ask."

Allison stayed in the common room for a long time, soaking in the warmth from the roaring fireplace and listening to the chatter of the other patrons. Everyone was talking about the riot that had almost been and Inspector Jairyn's crimes. There was even raucous laughter to go around, as they talked about how things might have gone without some timely intervention. They could laugh about it because it was all over. The mystery had been solved and the culprit had taken his own life rather than face the gallows. It was all over.

Near midnight, the door opened, drawing in errant flakes of snow that swirled about in the mingling of cold, winter wind from outside and fire-warmed air inside. It was Martin who came through the door, shaking snow from his cloak. He saw her almost at once and came directly to her table.

"Bloody-awful day," he said. "I hear you've settled things?"

"As much as they can be settled, I think," Allison replied tiredly.

"Ah, then you're not convinced, love? Everyone else seems to be, from what I can tell. Not that I've had much opportunity to be swapping stories with anybody. I've been holed up for nearly three days trying to maintain some order with the records. That, and helping to guard the cargo, what with everyone else all stirred up." He paused to thank Marcia as she brought around a stein of coffee for him. "But you think there might be more to the whole affair?"

"I've spent days wracking my brain," Allison said, "to no avail. The whole business with the slave trade, and that sham religion, have been put to rest, but...I don't know, Martin, a part of me thinks I ought to set aside whatever lingering questions I have and be satisfied with how things have turned out."

"And you keep wondering whether it's good enough for a detective to merely be 'satisfied,' is that it?" Martin asked.

Allison sighed. "Father would kill me if he were still alive to hear me suggest such a thing,"

"We all must do what we think right, love," Martin said stoically. "If you feel you've done enough, then you've done enough. If not...well...we're not going anywhere soon. But chin up, love, you've done a right fine job and there's no one in the town who'll argue otherwise."

"Thanks, Martin," Allison said. "You've been the one bright spot during this dreary affair." She drank deeply from her stein of coffee and felt all the lingering tension drain away at last. "You know, Martin, if the boat I took from Ellsberth hadn't sank, we could have gone out for a quiet sail in the harbor one day."

Martin laughed. "You've a strange idea of what constitutes a good time! But I'd have taken you up on the offer just the same, love."

"And if we could somehow find a day where the two of us aren't busy sunrise to sunset."

"Aye, and that."

Allison drank the last of her coffee, but continued to stare into the empty stein at the errant grounds stuck to the bottom. "I'll be glad to leave Illdara, Martin, I've no love for this cold."

"Nor I."

Following the end of the riot, tempers in the city cooled. Allison spent much of her time helping to oversee the various ongoing investigations in the city, of which there were a surprising many. Nothing on the scale of murder, but more than enough little things to keep her busy. When she was not doing that, she was helping to maintain calm relations between the natives of Illdara and the ship crews waiting out winter to bring the first shipments of gold south. Martin's help, in the case of the latter, was greatly appreciated. In the case of the former, Constable Wilminson's help proved invaluable. He knew much about the city and commanded a great deal of respect from citizens and sailors alike. He'd make chief inspector one day, if he accepted.

Winter in Illdara ended early, just four months after Allison's arrival. A miracle, some went so far as to say. The thick blanket of snow seemed to melt almost overnight as a warm, full sun appeared in the skies above the city. The coach, driven by that strange, old man, came down through the mountains just two days after the thaw.

Allison remembered the words of Albert Brimley, that Illdara was a hard place to leave, so she packed up all her things as quickly as could be managed. Though she did take extra care with all the documents and other evidence she'd uncovered related to the slave trade. With this done, she hurried downstairs, thanked Marcia for everything, and then went out to meet the coach. She loaded her bags and luggage and then opened the door to get in.

"You were going to leave without saying goodbye?"

Martin stood in the entrance to the inn, leaning against the door jam and breathing heavily.

"I suppose I got a little too caught up in heading back to the world," Allison said, smiling wryly. "But I should thank you for everything, if nothing else."

Martin shrugged. "It was fun, love, even I'll admit that."

"Will you come with me to the capital, Martin? You spoke so much about how you wanted to see it someday."

He thought on this, long and hard. Then he shook his head. "I want to, love, but I just can't, not right now. Maybe someday, when I'm not too busy with some other fool thing, I'll come find you."

"That's where I'll be," Allison said. She turned to get in the coach, but stopped. "Martin, is that really all you're going to leave me with? Surely there's more, something that you can't quite find the words to say aloud?"

His face flushed slightly and he produced a letter from one of his pockets. "You were so quick to leave and I hadn't even thought of what to say when you finally did. I wrote this up real quick, love, so don't judge too harshly. But how did you know?"

Allison took the letter and then carefully turned his hands over. His fingers were smudged with ink.

"A hunch, Martin, that's all," she said.

He laughed at that.

Allison unfolded the letter as she walked back to the carriage. It was written in such haste that the letters were shaky and lopsided. He talked about the brief time they'd spent together and of his hopes to see the capital one day, he even hinted at his hopes that their relationship might deepen, if they were able to meet again. Allison stopped, one boot resting on the bottom step. There was more on the page and another besides, but Allison had already seen enough.

"You know, Martin," Allison said, "I'd always thought it might be possible, but I never wanted to believe it."

"What do you mean?" he asked, still smiling.

She turned to look him in the eye. "You did well in hiding your voice and your writing, but not well enough."

"I see." He sighed, his shoulders slumping as if a weight pressed down on them. Then he chuckled to himself, as if at a private joke. "You're clever, love, more clever than I."

Allison drew her pistol and held it pointed at his heart. "Don't try to run, Martin, I'd rather not hurt you."

"So, you aren't going to let this go, are you? Look, I did the only thing I knew how to do. They were all on their deathbeds, dying with their lives unfulfilled as they waited to be taken by an unbearable pain. Inspector Jairyn? Can you even comprehend the suffering that has been endured at his hands? It had to stop, love, one way or another. It had to stop. Be satisfied with knowing you've helped put an end to that."

Allison slowly shook her head. "Its like you said, Martin, I've got to do what I think best. I'm my father's daughter, after all, and he taught me well. Now, come with me to the capital."

"You know I can't."

Allison slid back the hammer with her thumb.

"We bet it all on you being a good detective, tenacious to a fault," Martin said, "like your father. You exceeded both our expectations."

"Victoria?"

His smile this time was different, filled with a deep melancholy. "I wish you could have met her, love."

Then he turned and ran. The hammer slammed forward.

Epilogue

A coach pulled by two stout horses worked its way through the mountains. Fog hung thick in the air, obscuring everything more than twenty feet away and muffling the dull *clop* of the horses' hooves. Illdara was a day behind and there was still at least another day yet to go before the mountains parted, revealing gently-rolling plains. The driver sat hunched in his seat, cloak wrapped tightly around his shoulders against the cool, wet air, holding the reigns limply in his hands. The horses knew the way well enough.

Allison had changed since first coming to Illdara, no question of that. She felt more sure of herself, more determined than ever before to ensure that each case she came across ended with the culprit being taken into custody. The images of her father lingered, images of him when he was still alive and images of him in death. There would always be that danger when it came to solving the crime of murder, because one who has killed once has little left to lose by killing again, but she no longer felt that hesitance, that fear that could freeze her in her tracks. She finally knew what it was that her father had faced every day. Even so, it felt as though a piece of her had been left behind in Illdara, a piece that she would never get back.

"Is the capital really as beautiful as they say?"

Martin was laid flat on the seat opposite Allison, his right shoulder held in a rough sling and his face still pale from all the blood he'd lost. His feet were chained to the floor of the coach.

"Even more beautiful," Allison said. "We'll be there soon and you can see it for yourself."

"I can't wait."

The End

Made in the USA
Las Vegas, NV
08 December 2023

82312847R00105